Praise for // Lost in Found Footage

"*The Final Girls* for found footage! Pokes fun at all the tropes while also telling a solid horror story and doing the sub-genre justice."

-Anthony Cousins, director of *Frogman* & *Frogman Returns*

"An amazing love letter to meta horror and found footage, where all the familiar tropes we enjoy are there, but it doesn't feel hackneyed or phoned in. Powell's love of horror, and especially found footage, is profoundly clear from the jump. This is Joey Powell's best, most fun book yet."

-T.T. Madden, lead writer of *Hunt a Killer: Blair Witch*

"Powell delivers once again with his trademark style blend of horror, humor, and heart. *Lost In Found Footage* throws us right into the overly-meta world we live in now, where we've seen all the horror movies, and know all the tropes and can call every bad decision a character is going to make from a mile away. It's fast-paced with rounded, well written characters and a fun nod to the found footage movies we've all seen before."

-A.D. Aro, author of the *Bumps in the Night* series

"Reads like Goosebumps for adults. Lovers of *The Blair Witch Project* and other analogue-based horror movies, this one is for you."

-Marissa Yarrow, author of *Island X*

"Not only an homage to the film genre it parodies, *Lost in Found Footage* subtly explores themes of identity and self-worth. Joey Powell continues to be one of the most talented indie horror writers of his contemporaries. His style is often casual yet purposeful, and the stories are always layered."

-Jesse's House of Pulp

"*Lost in Found Footage* is an ode to found footage horror that understands exactly why the subgenere continues to captivate audiences. More than emulating familiar tropes, Powell crafts a metafictional horror story that examines what happens when a devoted fan goes from watching horror and is forced to survive it."

-Abby Wolf, book critic for *Cemetary Dance*

LOST IN FOUND FOOTAGE

JOEY POWELL

MAD AXE MEDIA

MADAXEMEDIA.COM

Book Cover by Joey Powell

Paperback ISBN: 978-1-966497-28-8

Ebook ISBN: 978-1-966497-29-5

LOST IN FOUND FOOTAGE

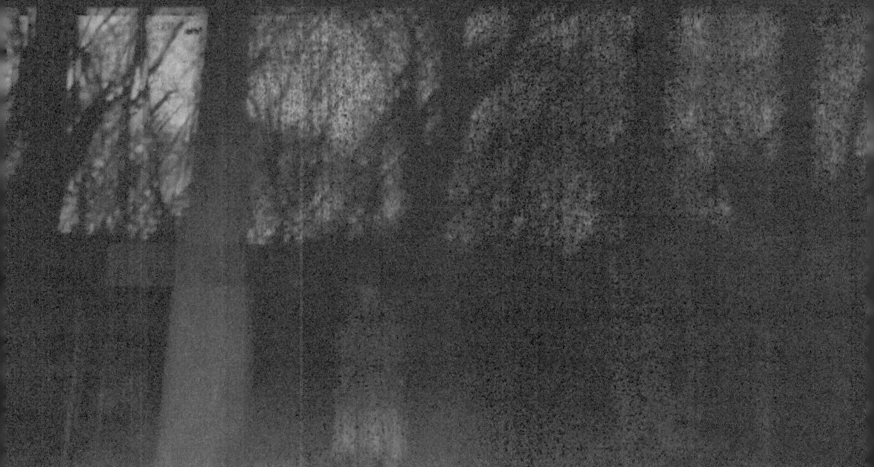

THE CAMERA

"HEY, MAN, CAN YOU say *exactly* what you just said a couple seconds ago into the camera? It'd look so good for my video."

Grey Carter had just found the perfect video camera: A mini-DV with a velcro strap on the right side that his fingers slid perfectly into. Dull silver with scuff marks around the hardened plastic exterior. So lightweight. So digital.

He popped open the viewfinder, careful not to move too fast; there was no telling how long this thing could last. It wasn't the battery life he was worried about, but rather the mechanics of the thing. The insides *whirred* in a way he didn't quite remember his old DV camera doing way back when he was fifteen. The one held in his hand droned on in this grinding cadence as if the DV tape inside of it was filled with rocks instead of celluloid.

But this beautiful specimen—doomed as it may have been—was very special to Grey on this night in particular.

Tonight, Grey would be attending a screening of a new found footage movie.

"What would you like me to say?" the pawn shop clerk asked, his disinterested face and donut-shaped tuft of hair captured in the viewfinder of Grey's new (old-as-shit) camera. The light from the window behind him was blown out completely as captured on video, creating an angelic digital glow around the man's body.

"Bro, the thing you just said about the camera being haunted or whatever," Grey said. "And if you could do it in, like, an ominous voice, that'd be so chill."

The old man sighed. "What I said was—"

"Oh, wait!" Grey pressed the record button, only to realize he'd been recording the entire exchange. He pressed it again, starting the recording intentionally this time. "Just, uh, had to make sure I was recording. Go ahead."

"All I said was a guy came in—this real tall, lanky fella—and dumped the camera off without asking for any payment. All he said was whoever got the camera next would become the subject of their own film."

Grey gave his voice a cartoonish inflection. "*Would become the subject of their own film, oo-hoo-hoooo.* Could you try it like that?"

The store clerk walked toward the front door. "I do hope you enjoy your purchase, sir."

Grey stopped recording and closed the viewfinder. "I was just havin' a little fun, man. I'm goin' to a movie screening tonight. Thought it would be cool to vlog the ex—never mind." The guy was likely in his fifties and managed a pawn shop. What care would he have to give?

It *was* fun, though. Even as the camera dangled in his grip, with his fingers wedged between the strap and the rough exterior, memories flooded his mind of making home videos with neighborhood friends. First, it was improvised scenes with a loose outline of a movie. Then, it was written outlines. Then, it was full scripts.

But that was back when his friends had a lot more time and far more imagination. Before everyone traded in their basketball shorts for khakis, their tank tops for dress shirts. Before everyone found success doing unfulfilling things, and Grey chased a fulfilling dream, only to realize too late that it was out of reach.

Oh well.

He was a decent-ish content creator, so in a way, he was still holding onto that dream, even if he was at the whims of algorithms owned by corporations and mobile apps that were constantly at risk of being either shut down or taken over by eighty-year-old politicians.

"Hope you enjoy your movie," the store clerk said as Grey walked past. "What are you seeing?"

"*The Witch of Hope Hollow*," Grey said. "It's a found footage movie."

"Who found the footage?"

"No, that's not ... It's, like, somebody shot the footage, usually on a camera like this one, and then it was found. It's a framing device."

"You're going to a theater to see a movie shot on a camera like *that?*" the store clerk asked while eyeing the device he'd just sold to Grey.

"Yeah, it's gonna look terrible judging by the trailers."

The old man raised his eyebrows and shrugged.

It was a reasonable reaction.

THE VAGABOND

"HEY, GUYS, SO, FOUND footage movies. What's the deal, right? Everyone thought the trend would die out, but they're still getting made *and* distributed. Why? Because they're easy to shoot! See what I'm doing right now? Just talking straight into the camera explaining what I'm doing? *This* could be the beginning of a found footage movie. No joke, it's that simple. And how many found footage movies have you seen centered around social media influencers going into some haunted house or something? Well ... I *am* a content creator ... and I *do* have a cursed camera ... I think we have our setup, lads."

Grey stopped recording and closed the viewfinder. That was enough for now. By his estimation, he had about one minute of edited content already, which meant he'd need another nine to max out the monetization opportunities for his video. This was the way his brain worked now. Even as he walked into the sunset of Parkwood Avenue, gazing into the Downtown Raleigh skyline as the last rays of sunlight streaked through the edges of skyscrapers, all he could think about was the construction of his videos. How to maximize profit. How to get any profit whatsoever. It wasn't the life he'd hoped for.

Some days, a video would explode. The engagement would flood in, prompting a delightful surge of dopamine.

Other days, the views and comments would lag.

Rarely did he understand how or why some content performed better than others. It was a constant guessing game. He'd followed trends and tried to predict popularity until his efforts washed out all artistic merit, and he became a shell of the "filmmaker" he wanted to be.

A muffled chime sounded from the phone. He slid his free hand into his pocket to check it.

A YouTube comment on his last video read:

RollingShutter459: "Weak analysis. No mention of *Annihilation* as modern cosmic horror. You should invest in better lighting equipment as well. Very amateur. This channel should die."

RollingShutter459 was a YouTube account with no videos and no playlists, only a long history of angry comments accompanied by a thumbnail of a 16mm camera. Accounts like this one seemed to pour all of their ire into Grey's content, further bruising his already rotted ego. To be called an amateur was to have his cool content creator mask ripped clean off by someone who knew how Grey really felt about himself down to his core, down to his bones. Truth inside of an insult.

People online can be such assholes.

"Careful with that thing." A gruff voice snapped Grey out of his dour stupor.

Grey craned his neck toward the footsteps that followed behind him. A tall, slender man, barefoot and with loose pants dangling from his bony legs, approached Grey. A hoodie covered the top half of the man's face so that all Grey could make out by way of facial features was the scraggly beard hanging over the tall man's chest.

"Careful with what?" Grey asked.

"The camera you just purchased." The tall man stopped in front of him. A waft of musk surrounded his unkempt appearance. "I was lucky enough to escape it," the man whispered, "but the device required a new subject. I'm ... I'm so very sorry."

"Wait ... were you the guy who left this at the pawn shop?" Grey asked.

Were Grey a superstitious man, he may have been more attentive to the genuine guilt and terror slathered over the man's dry skin, his sad, hollow pits of eyes. He would have understood the man's warning to be authentic—an act of mercy.

But Grey wasn't superstitious. He was a creator. And this was content gold.

Grey raised the camera, flipped open the viewfinder, and pressed the record button as fast as his thumb could manage. "Can you say all that again for the camera? Exactly how you just said it?"

"You don't realize what's coming," the man said.

Grey's eyes drifted from the man in front of him to the viewfinder. It captured the full environment in the camera's frame—the sidewalk, the stained buildings, the cars drifting past—but not the subject of the frame himself. Instead, the tall man was a digital glitch in the outline of a human being. Particles of reds and greens and yellows danced alongside each other in place of the figure, without a single true-to-life feature captured within the lens of the camera.

"There's something wrong with this thing," Grey said to himself.

"The device has had me already. I'm no longer of use to it."

That's quite the trick, Grey thought, though his mind raced in circles trying to figure out how the hell—*heck*—the guy could have rigged the camera to do it. A magnetic vest underneath his hood that degraded the video input? But why? Just for shits and giggs?

"Once the device is activated," the man said, "the only way out is to complete the film."

Okay, I'll play along, Grey thought. The video might have been degraded, but he was still getting the audio. "How is it activated?"

The man's eyes lowered to the ground. "Good luck."

He turned toward the street and took three heavy steps across the pavement before Grey registered that he was walking straight into traffic.

"No-no-no, wait!" Grey shouted as a car horn blasted. A sedan came to a screeching halt mere inches from the unflinching pedestrian.

But the man continued walking.

"Whoa," Grey said before turning the camera back on himself and speaking into it. "That was intense. Will I get cursed by the camera? Let's find out." He winked. "The guy's fine, by the way. He made it across the road."

He turned the camera off and continued walking.

THE TRINKET

"WHOA, THIS IS SO cool!" Michael said as he eyed the video camera orbiting around in his hands.

It must have appeared so foreign to him, what with all the buttons on the side, the flip-out viewfinder on the other. At eight years old, Michael had never seen a device that could record video without a touch screen. At least, not in real life. Michael's father had let him watch *The Blair Witch Project* as part of a Halloween movie marathon on basic cable, something that Cassandra, Grey's older sister, was not too happy about. She'd expected nightmares, but instead, Michael came back to her that weekend with a newfound interest in horror movies. "I want to be a horror filmmaker like Uncle Grey," he'd said.

"I'm using it for my next video," Grey said proudly. "Your idea, remember?"

A glimmer of excitement splashed across Michael's face. "Really?!"

"Yeah, the video's gonna be dedicated to you, my little found footage guru."

"You're gonna shoot it like the *Blair Witch Project*?"

"I sure am." Grey grinned. "Oh, and guess what ... The guy who sold it to me said this camera ..." He raised his hands for emphasis. "... is cursed. Don't tell your mom."

Michael put his index finger on his lips and grinned.

A clatter from the kitchen caused Grey to jolt upright on the couch. "Shit," Grey said instinctively, forgetting Cassandra's no cursing rule. Shards of porcelain spilled across the tile flooring, the dinner plate a casualty of Cassandra emptying the dishwasher too quickly.

"Oh, f—" Cassandra caught herself. "*Fudge.*"

"Shit!" Michael exclaimed, parroting Grey.

Cassandra looked from the broken plate into the living room, staring daggers into Grey. "Thanks for that."

"Shit!" Michael said again.

"Hey, buddy," Grey said, touching the boy's shoulder, "we're not supposed to say that, okay? Uncle Grey had a slip-up." Grey met Cassandra's stare again. "And he's *very* sorry."

Cassandra rolled her eyes. She was doing better with her language, and Grey had all the admiration in the world for his sister's transition from wild, hard-partying twenty-something to clean-cut mom. While Grey spent the bulk of his twenties chasing dreams and succumbing to false starts, Cassandra found herself with the demands that come with an unplanned pregnancy. Even worse, it was with someone she wouldn't pick out of a police interrogation lineup to be the father of her child. But she'd stepped up.

When it came to being an uncle, Grey stepped up in his own way. He provided a distraction. Some relief for his sister, who seemed to be constantly drowning while juggling work, childcare coordination, parenting, exercising, and maybe some sleep every once in a while. She needed more from Grey, and he knew it. To Cassandra, a distraction wasn't good enough. Michael needed a father figure.

But Grey would never choose to be someone's father figure. It was never his desire. And he certainly wasn't in a position to be needed by someone else. The calls from Cassandra crying late at night had stopped a few years ago, which, ironically, was right around the time that Michael was officially deemed by a physician as on the spectrum. It might've been because Michael was getting older. It might've been because Grey was too unreliable to trust. He looked back on those times and realized Cassandra wasn't calling to vent; she was calling for help. She just had too much pride to ask, and he was too stupid to read between the lines.

But he was a dreamer digging himself deeper into piles of debt, both carefree and careless. He wasn't in a position to help anyone. He couldn't even help himself.

He thought that maybe things would change by the time he rounded the corner on thirty, but even now as he showed off his shiny new toy, feeling flattered that his eight-year-old admirer thought it was cool and as Cassandra checked chores off from her list, he was content in only being a distraction, in keeping Michael calm for an hour.

Content.

"You need some help in there?" Grey called out, even though Cassandra was already in the process of sweeping the shards into a dust pan.

"Nope," she called back.

"Is Mom upset?" Michael asked Grey.

"Not at you, buddy," Grey replied. He checked his watch and realized it was getting close to the movie screening. "Okay, I have to go test out this fancy new camera. Can I have it back?"

"Can I have it when you're done?" Michael asked.

"Oo, depends on how ... *cursed* it is."

Michael giggled and handed Grey the camera. Once his hands were empty, he returned one to his pocket and trained his eyes downward sheepishly. "Okay, well ... I kinda want to give you something too."

"Oh yeah?" Grey inquired. "Whatcha got?" The kid could have handed him a marker sketch of a spider with a dog's head, and Grey would have considered it the greatest gift in the world.

Michael removed a circular brass object from his pocket and lowered his voice. "Mom's been getting outdoors stuff for me because I keep asking about Cub Scouts. She said I can do it soon, but I should practice for now ... I want you to have my compass."

The boy held it out for Grey, who gently plucked it out of his hand, eyeing the glass top and the rotating metal arm beneath it.

"Oh, buddy ... are you sure?" Grey asked.

"Mom said you're directionless. I thought it might help you."

A laugh crackled in Grey's throat. At first, it was an involuntary reaction to Michael's misunderstanding of Cassandra's figure of speech, which was indeed funny, but it continued on in an ironic way, trapped in a lackadaisical chuckle state. He knew Cassandra didn't think all that much of the life he'd made for himself, but hearing it out loud—from her child, no less—felt like an anvil thrown from Mount Everest.

Ego: *SPLAT.*

"Thanks, Mikey," Grey said. "I think you're right. This might just help me." He thumbed the smooth surface of the compass and put it in his jeans pocket. "I'll see you soon, big guy. Don't give your mom too much trouble, okay?"

Grey walked toward the kitchen as Cassandra returned from the laundry room, having disposed of the broken dish.

"Where are you going?" Cassandra asked.

"To a movie. I'm going to do this live reaction thing where I record myself going to the theater and coming out and whatnot. Totally Michael's idea. He's on YouTube a lot and sees other horror vloggers doing it, so he wanted me to give it a shot." As he spoke, Grey saw Cassandra's eyes glaze over, a look he mistook for boredom before realizing it was anger.

"You were gonna watch Michael tonight," Cassandra said. "Did you forget?"

"I—What? When did you tell me this?"

"I asked you last month if you could block out this night—*this* specific night."

"A month ago? That's, like ... really far in advance. It's hard for me to plan ahead like that. What, did you have something planned?"

Cassandra bit her lip so hard Grey thought it might bleed. The raw emotion accentuated the bags under her eyes that she concealed so well with makeup. "Forget it. It was just book club. Just a book club with some other women in the complex. Just wanted to feel human on a Friday night." She lowered her voice. "Just one fucking night out of the month."

"Oh, I can take him to the movie with me."

"What are you seeing? A horror movie?"

"Yeah."

"R-rated?"

"Yeah."

She laughed while gritting her teeth. "Never mind. Go see your movie. I'll stay here with Michael."

Grey knew that tone in Cassandra's voice. She was defeated, deflated, and, worst of all, disappointed. He had to fix this fast. "It's okay, I won't go. I'll hang back with Michael. You can go to your—"

"No, Grey. I don't *want* you to be with Michael tonight. It's clearly not something you can prioritize."

"But I'm offering to ditch the movie."

Cassandra tilted her head with a look that was almost pitying. "It's really sad that you can't see why that's an issue."

"Okay, I'm confused. I'm a really good uncle to that kid."

"You are," Cassandra agreed half heartedly. "I'll see you later, Grey." She walked to the door and opened it.

Grey said, "I'm dedicating the video to Mikey."

As if that meant anything to Cassandra.

THE THEATER

DAMN, I SHOULD HAVE stayed.

No—DANG, *I should have stayed.*

Did he actually think that "catch" just then was a positive step toward being a better uncle? Filtering no-no words was easy. Easier than keeping a schedule. He didn't remember Cassandra telling him to block out this Friday night—he really didn't—which meant she either: 1) Failed to mention it but thought she did; or 2) He failed to hear it.

But he'd offered to stay and she'd declined, so what was the point?

It was too late now, anyway. He was already at the Parkwood Theater, an old, graffiti-lined brick building on the outskirts of Downtown Raleigh. It had changed hands so many times, Grey's movie-loving heart feared it was on the brink of abandonment any day now. They had a knack for playing oddball films. Sure, they'd program the random awards contender here and there, but sometimes they'd screen silly B-movie goodness—the type of films that put the highest percentage of a very low budget into blood and gore effects.

On the nights he went to see such films, sometimes marveling and sometimes cringing at the sheer ingenuity of creation on screen, Grey imagined some crazy old guy in the projector booth with a huge grin plastered on his face. A man who perhaps owned VHS copies of *The Toxic Avenger* and various Troma films. He didn't know who owned the cinema now, and he didn't care to know. In his mind, it was best left as a mystery.

As was the theater's decision to program *The Witch of Hope Hollow*, a cheap—like, *mega*-cheap—found footage film that, judging by the trailers, appeared to be shot on a camcorder no more technologically advanced than the one Grey had just purchased. Grey had seen way too many found footage films, and he fully expected this one to follow the exact same run-and-gun, bare-bones structure:

1. Characters talk in blatant exposition on camera, achieving the minimum amount of character development, if any at all.

2. They travel to a new location to "investigate" something—bonus points if they're a documentary crew, which explains the camera being on the whole time.

3. They interview various townspeople about the something they're investigating.

4. Weird stuff happens, and we pad the runtime for about fifty minutes, until ...

5. All hell (and budget) breaks loose in the last ten minutes.

Would this one be any different?

Probably not.

It was following a different crew setting out to capture the Hope Hollow Witch on camera. But Grey was a horror guy. It was his niche. And his followers counted on him for his horror movie recommendations.

That's the thing about horror hounds—they can't get enough. There are hundreds of horror films being pumped out a year and hundreds watched. People love being scared. People love camp. People love seeing characters running for their lives or drenched in blood. Once upon a time, Grey would have been that filmmaker who brought such thrills to viewers, but for now, he'd have to settle for the somber realization that he, too, was a viewer.

A critic.

At least he was entertaining 600K people.

Don't forget to like and subscribe.

The ticket booth at Parkwood Theater had been vacant for years. It killed the reminiscent joy of seeing a kid in a colorful vest printing out tickets, just like 90s-Grey remembered. Instead, Grey had to walk into the lobby, camera raised, and get a ticket printed from—

Oh, shit. Not this fu—uuuhhh, frickin'—*guy. Language, Grey, language.*

Grey had known Rodney for half his life. He'd had long black hair tied back in a ponytail when Grey had first met him back in high school in the Film and TV club, and that same ponytail presently tracked dandruff onto the back of his "Parkwood Theater" vest. Between the hair and a face riddled with pimples, Rodney was in serious need of a geek-to-glam makeover.

"You can't bring that in here," Rodney said, looking at the camera.

"It's for my channel," Grey responded. "I just want people to get a feel for the theater-going experience here. Don't you want me to promote the theater to my millions of followers?"

"You don't have *millions* of followers," Rodney said with a stone-cold expression.

"So you *have* seen my channel!"

Rodney's eyes drifted for a moment before returning to Grey. "It's illegal for you to smuggle a camera into a theater."

Sometimes Grey would walk into the theater and see some fresh-faced clock-watcher kid who didn't care much about the job besides the measly paycheck, but now he was standing in the lobby with the same guy who NARC'ed on him two months ago for bringing in his own store-bought box of candy. Rodney was *serious* about the job and upholding Parkwood Theater's policies, which made sense considering his father was the owner.

"How's your dad?" Grey asked. "I haven't seen him here in a while."

"He's been sick," Rodney said plainly.

"For how long? Like, is it serious?"

"Why do you wanna know?"

"I've been going to this theater for two decades, man, I just wanna know if he's okay."

"He's fine. Probably."

That pause before "probably" was so subtle yet so ominous to Grey. It was almost as if Rodney had meant to emphasize the ambiguity of his father's physical wellbeing.

"Could you tell him that I wish him well?" Grey asked.

"He's not gonna know who you are."

That was a lie.

When they were in high school, Grey and Rodney would shoot their version of "films" all over town, sometimes using this exact theater as a set. Rodney's father would let them screen their movies in the theater. Rodney was such a shy kid back then, and Grey assumed all he wanted to was to be involved. Since he rarely spoke, he was typically relegated to holding the boom mic.

Nowadays, he seemed to *really* despise Grey.

In a curt tone, Rodney said, "Now, *sir*, if you wouldn't mind—"

"Okay, okay, I'll take it back to my car," Grey said. Except there was no car. Grey had walked there, which Rodney couldn't have known. With the camera still raised, Grey said, "One ticket for—"

"You don't have my consent to capture my likeness on camera," Rodney blurted.

"Whoa, relax, Rodney. One ticket for the *Witch of Hope Hollow*, please."

Rodney's demeanor shifted. He stiffened. His face of stone turned even more stern than Grey thought possible. Even the degraded and pixelated view of the camcorder caught the downward slant in the groves of his cheeks and mouth. "Are you ... sure ... you want to buy a ticket to that movie?"

"Um ... yeah, I'm sure," Grey answered.

Rodney leaned over the concession stand, eyeing the camera lens intently, and lowered his voice. "You know ... I hear that movie is ..." His eyes darted left, then right. "... cursed."

A childlike joy rose in Grey's stomach. "Oh, really? How so?"

"Well ... not too many people have come to see it, but the ones who do come out of the theater ... *changed.* We've gone through three different projectors since we started playing it."

"No way. Like, three different physical projectors or three people who work the projectors?"

"Don't go see this film ... You may not survive it ..." Rodney shifted away from the camera.

Yes! This was exactly what Grey needed for his review. This was going to be—

"Too bad you can't use that footage. You know, since I didn't provide consent, and all," Rodney said in a monotone affectation.

"Oh, come on," Grey stopped recording and lowered the camera. "You were playing me?"

"That is correct. Now, please remove the camera from your person, and you may purchase a ticket."

"Ah, fine."

THE WARP

IT WAS EASY ENOUGH to sneak the camera in. The thing was slightly bigger than two softballs, and Grey's pants had wide enough legs to conceal it, so when Grey stepped outside and rummaged around the parking lot pretending to go back to his car, he simply stuffed the camera into his tube sock and unrolled his pant leg back over it. As long as he walked slowly, the thing wouldn't come flying out.

As expected, he was the only one in the theater that evening. A plastic-tombstone-laden graveyard lay beneath the screen from his back-row view. The appetite for this scrappy found footage movie seemed to be minimal at best, and, once again, he found himself wondering why Parkwood would set money on fire to screen this film. All the better for him, though, since he could record his live reaction.

"Okay, so the movie just started," Grey said into the camera. "We're getting the obligatory meet-the-characters stuff. Honestly, I'm not sure if this is all improvised or if they're just bad actors. So far, we have Larry, who's this wannabe documentarian professor at a film school. He's recruited a crew of scrappy students to go shoot a doc about the Witch. There's some allusion to him having had some kind of hush-hush relationship with Blaire, who's running sound. Or maybe it's a crush. It seems like he's only slightly older than her, so not a huge deal, but, hey, expect that to come back in the climax when they're running for their lives, right? There's Johnson, who's the 'producer' or whatever. They actually have a line where someone says, 'What do you do?' He's obviously there to crack jokes. He'll probably be the audience surrogate. And then we have the cameraman. They haven't said his name yet—"

The double doors squeaked open.

Oh, shoot. Grey instinctively hid the camera by wedging it between his leg and the right arm rest. Who could have been walking into a movie ten minutes late?

Slow footsteps trickled in.

Rodney's sneakers pattered on the carpet as he pretended to inspect the theater. It was clear, though, that he'd come just to make Grey sweat. He knew Grey wouldn't follow his rules.

His eyes landed on Grey, who was doing his best to look inconspicuous, putting his forearm over the top of the camera.

For reasons Grey couldn't understand, Rodney walked into Grey's row and took a seat next to him, unfolding the old-school movie theater chair and parking himself on the stained cushion.

After an uncomfortably long moment of silence, Grey said, "Careful ... I hear this movie's cursed."

"I've seen it," Rodney said, keeping his eyes on the screen as the film played on. "A few times, actually. Every time, the theater was empty."

"It can't be profitable to keep this thing on your screens."

"I fought Dad on it. He doesn't like horror. Says nobody in town likes horror. He told me he'd reserve a screen for it for one week. Just for me. Even though he knows it won't make any money."

"That's ... nice. I mean, that's nice, right?"

Rodney ignored the question. "I watch movies like this, and ... I know they're not very good, but it's inspiring. These people with so little resources went out and just made something. They had a love for the genre, a love for the craft, and just ... did it."

Grey could sense the sadness in Rodney's tone, like he was mourning a path never taken. A pile of rocks sank in Grey's stomach as he realized he and Rodney weren't all that different. They'd been on the same trajectory once. Things didn't pan out for either of them.

The sudden vulnerability was so awkward for Grey that all he could say was, "Yeah, it's pretty inspiring, man. I agree." Another long moment of silence followed as they both watched the characters on screen drive around the middle-of-nowhere town commenting on how desolate the place looked. They slowed to a stop at a stop sign with a spray painted message that read:

THE WITCH LIVES

"Why don't you just make a movie?" Grey said. "Do something like this?"

Rodney shook his head. "It's too late."

"What are you talking about? I mean—" *Don't say it, Grey.* "—I have equipment." *Stop. Leave it at that.* "Maybe—" *No!* "—we could make something."

Rodney grunted. He lowered his voice. "You would use me for my dad's resources again."

"What? We never—"

"Never what? Took any of my ideas?

"Any of your ideas? You never spoke."

"You never listened."

"Dude, where is this coming from?"

Rodney gave a short, mocking laugh. "Make a movie together. You an I … We're both fucking losers."

"Rodney—"

"That's not even my name!"

He turned in seat so quickly and so angrily that it made Grey jump and raise his arms. Grey fully expected Rodney—or *not* Rodney—to smack him.

In that split second, the light from the screen hit the top of the camera. Rodney looked down across Grey's lap.

"I *told you* not to bring that in. I'll have to confiscate that piece of equipment to ensure no portion of the film was recorded."

"I didn't record the movie, man!" Grey said, still bracing for impact. "Just my reaction."

"Then you captured some of the audio, which is also illegal, dumbass."

"It's a grey area." *Grey Area*, he thought. *That's what I should have named my channel …*

Rodney reached across Grey's chest, his dry, crusty fingers zeroing in on the camera.

"Dude, chill!" Grey yelled. "Let's just talk this out! What's your actual name?!"

Rodney refused to chill. "Give it! Give it!"

Grey struggled for control as Rodney's hands found the camera.

But as he tried to stand, Rodney tripped, sending their joint momentum to the ground and the camera out of his grasp.

Still recording, the camera took two hard skips on the floor before skidding into the carpeted aisle, the lens aimed directly at the screen as *The Witch of Hope Hollow* continued playing.

"What is your problem?!" Grey shrieked, hoping the camera wasn't damaged, but expecting that it was.

Before Grey got his elbows underneath him, Rodney picked himself up with swift athleticism betrayed by his goofy appearance. He headed for the camera.

"If that thing's broken, man ..." Grey said.

The side wall closest to the camera *flickered* ... It was the only way Grey could have described it to somebody, if only to laugh about what he *thought* he saw. Surely, he hadn't seen the red, green, and blue paint shift into dissecting bars under the dim theater lights.

Surely, he hadn't seen the wall ...

Glitch.

But Rodney was frozen in his tracks, stalled in his pursuit of the illegal device Grey had smuggled into the theater. Grey thought for a moment that maybe his foe had seen the glitch, too.

Then, that same flicker turned a row of seats into temporary digitized ribbons.

Rodney whispered, "What ... the ..."

So he *was* seeing it.

Suddenly, a vortex of pixelated light, twisting and shrinking, consumed the theater, reducing the walls, the ceiling, and the floor to a rainbow cavalcade of particles.

Before Grey had a chance to realize that he, too, had become a cluster of pixels at the whims of the vortex, he was swallowed by its light.

Brilliant …

Vibrant …

Terrifying light.

The Witch of Hope Hollow
Timecode: 08:12:03

Larry Baxter sets his bag down in the rental cabin, then looks into the camera and says, "Keep it rolling, Caleb. I want to capture as much of this trip as we can."

"I got the back-up batteries all juiced up, boss. We're good to go here," the voice behind the camera says.

Larry nods and turns. The camera rotates, revealing Caleb, its operator, a fresh-faced, older-than-he-looks kid in his twenties, smirking. He places the fingertips of his straightened freehand to the front of his beanie and salutes, mouthing *Yessir* before putting the camera back on Larry.

Larry leads Caleb through the hallway, across the living room, and out toward the back patio, which overlooks a wooded area with spikes of sunlight streaking through the limbs. Larry raises his hands and forms an invisible frame. "This would make a great shot," he prompts Caleb.

"Oh, soOOoo cinematic," Blaire chides from behind them.

Larry's hands drop. He turns around and laughs. "We want this thing to look good, right?"

A clatter from inside the house *JOLTS* the trio, prompting Blaire to spin and peer behind her. Johnson, looking like an extra in a high school football drama with his tall, bulky frame, approaches them on the patio, leaving behind a nylon bag filled with something heavy enough to make a loud clatter when dropped. "Could you be careful with that?" Caleb asks. "Why don't you go make up the beds or something?"

"It belongs to the school," Johnson says. "It's insured. And I'll make *my* bed. I got top bunk."

"Hell no," Caleb retorts. "I ain't riskin' all 250 pounds of you crushin' my ass in my sleep tonight. I'll gladly take top bunk. And, by the way …" Caleb pans the camera over to Larry. "... this guy works for the school, remember?"

"Yeah, dumbass," Blaire says. "If you're gonna mishandle the equipment, maybe don't do it within earshot of him."

"Oh, right," Johnson laughs nervously. "My bad. I forget sometimes because you seem, like, you know… one of us. How old are you again?"

Larry chuckles. "I don't think that's an appropriate question."

"Thirty," Blaire blurts. "So, night on the town?"

"Drinks on Professor Baxter," Johnson says.

"Hey, I might *seem* like one of you, but Blaire's the only one out of all of you who's twenty-one. Besides, I have a special surprise."

"Oo, do tell …" Blaire says.

"The reason I booked us this cabin is that it's in close proximity to the Witch's house."

"The Witch's house doesn't exist, man," Caleb says from behind the camera. "The town demolished it."

"But, according to myth, it appears to those who seek it," Larry says. "We're out here seeking it, aren't we?"

"Solid point, my dude," Johnson says. "Oh, damn, I think I left my tin foil hat back in the dorm. Do you have an extra one, Larry?"

Larry continues, ignoring the question. "It's about ten miles north of this cabin. I say we take a little trip through the woods and … see if anything weird happens."

"Like, a house just *appearing* out of thin air?" Blaire asks.

"I'll bring all the backup batteries," Caleb says, "The sun's going to be down soon, and the flashlight drains the battery on this thing real quick."

"Did anyone bring flashlights?" Blaire asks.

"No, why would we bring flashlights?" Johnson asks. "We *literally* have a camera with a flashlight on it. Smarter, not harder, sweets."

THE DANGER

WHAT THE SHIZZ WAS *that?* The words pulsed through Grey's brain, sending shockwaves through his milky, incoherent vision. *Did someone drug me? Was it that little theater pipsqueak?*

The last thing he remembered was the screening room transforming into bright lights, almost like a rave dropped acid then sneezed. He remembered his body being lifted off the ground—not pulled by anything tangible, but rather like the gravitational shift of a tornado. He was Bill Paxton and Helen Hunt at the end of *Twister* without the damn leather belt to keep him on the ground.

But wherever that twister had carried him to, it wasn't another spot in the theater. His body was no longer lying across a floor sticky with spilled soda and coated in butter salt. Several little needles poked at his sides, under the exposed skin of his arms.

No, not needles. That smell ...

It was grass.

Blades of hard, dry grass.

Grey lifted himself to his feet, scratching at his irritated skin. A full moon pierced through the dark clouds above him, offering just enough light to make out his surroundings as he scanned through a thick cluster of trees lining the grassy perimeter.

His eyes landed on a moss-covered stone structure, with mortar loose enough in spots to make it appear as if it might topple over if not bound together by a network of vines. The structure stood two stories high, its bottom half engulfed in vegetation, having become one with the forest long, long ago.

"Where the hell am I?" Grey whispered.

Aches and pains crept in, radiating through his bones as if he'd been flipped and tossed around like a tennis shoe in a dryer.

He reached down for his phone ...

Gone. Whatever had happened must've jostled it out of his pocket.

But then, his hand felt something else. Something small and smooth and he hoped wasn't damaged. He pulled Michael's compass out of his pocket, timidly inspecting the glass surface. Moonglow bounced off the surface, casting enough light for him to see the arrow pointing toward the big N, which formed a line straight to the foreboding stone house.

At least he knew he was northbound.

"Uh-Uh-Uh-Uh-Uh." A soft whimper echoed through the woods.

Grey whipped his head around, trying to identify where the sound was coming from ...

Until a sharp *CLACK* against the roof pulled his attention back to the structure, where he laid his eyes on something unconscionable. Something he wouldn't allow his mind to conceive of, even after he'd witnessed a room digitize and burst into light like a twenty-second-century simulation sparking in a microwave. Because there was no way in hell he was staring at a woman in a ripped and mud-stained white cloth dress, gripping the roof with her toes.

No ...

Not toes ...

Talons.

A sudden gust of wind raised the black, frayed hair obscuring her face and revealing a mouth that was sealed shut, with a rugged burn mark running from one cheek to the other, replacing the lips she had presumably once had.

Frozen in place, Grey gazed into the woman's bulging black eyes as a frequency of hums escaped her throat.

Two thin planes of bone and flesh and veins expanded behind the whimpering woman, revealing a set of wings flanking either side of her.

In a split second, she was off the roof, her wings carrying her higher into the moonlight.

"Shit ..." Grey said, forcing his body to move. His eyes darted to the ground, searching for anything he could use to defend himself with. It was the woods, wasn't it? There had to be a big goddamn stick lying around. Something he could get his hands on before that thing—

As soon as he looked up, the winged woman dive-bombed toward him.

"Shitshitshitshitshit!" Grey leaped out of her path, catching his weight in his sweaty palms and rolling into a clumsy somersault.

The woman disappeared into the woods, the blue moon-lit glow along her backside disappearing with her.

Grey knew that wasn't the last of her. Couldn't have been. His hands rummaged through the grass again for a stick, a twig, anything—until his fingers brushed against something thick, rough, and (hopefully) sturdy.

This something would have to do.

He lifted the branch and swung around to find wherever the woman was flying in from.

Two outstretched, mustard-colored talons filled his vision, claws ready to pierce his skin and lift him away.

The branch caught the woman's stomach before she could reach Grey. She *screeched* as he stumbled backward. The branch slipped from his grip, but stayed in her stomach.

A claw scraped across Grey's chest as the bird-woman flew past him, the angle of her descent causing the free end of the branch to snag the ground, further burying the impaled end into her midsection.

Painful shrieks bounced from tree to tree, reverberating through the forest as Grey clutched the gash in his chest, his adrenaline doing very little to lessen the burning of his exposed flesh.

The bird woman flailed on the ground, swinging the branch and slapping the dirt with each roll of her body. She flapped her wings, bringing herself a few feet off the ground, before collapsing in a pitiful mound of discolored white fabric and blood.

Grey knew that she was dying, but she was also working very hard at staying alive, and he didn't plan on sticking around to see if she'd kill him before she did.

He sprinted away from the woman, away from the stone house, exposing himself to whatever elements awaited him in this foreign place.

Panting, he wheezed, “Where...” *Pant.* “... the hell ...” *Pant.* “... Am—”

SMACK.

The world went black.

THE CAST

"HELLO?" A CALM VOICE called out. "Sir, are you okay?"

A flashlight sent glowing daggers through Grey's eye sockets as he tried to recover from what felt like the most aggressive hangover of his life. He held up a hand and mustered a hoarse response. "Wha ... What?"

That throbbing on his cheek could only have been a branch. While Grey was laser-focused on not twisting his ankle like a teenager in a slasher movie, he failed to notice this one giant asshole of a limb hanging just around the level of his forehead.

"Do you need medical attention, sir?" the voice said again as a clatter of footsteps mashed the dried grass in his periphery.

Grey sat up, shielding his face from the light, separating him from whomever was behind it. "Probably ... and some clothes, if you got any."

"Just got the clothes we have on us, friend. What are you doing out here?" A different voice this time. Deeper.

A flood of images poured back into Grey's brain.

The theater bursting into a cosmic vortex.

The demon-woman-thing diving toward him, nails out.

A claw removing a line of skin from his chest.

"We have to get outta here," Grey said, stumbling as he stood, shielding his face from the light.

"Whoa, buddy," the guy behind the light said, reacting to Grey's bloody chest. "That's a lot of red on ya."

"Could you lower that flashlight?" Grey asked. "It's giving me a headache."

As the cone of light came to a stop near its wielder's waist, Grey realized it wasn't a flashlight at all but rather a camera light. The cameraman, a fresh-faced twenty-something with a beanie, held the camera similarly to how a 1950s gangster held a Tommy gun, making sure the light stayed in front of him.

Grey squinted his eyes, looking past the cameraman to get a better view of the rest of the group. A tall, stalky guy with sharp cheekbones held his broad jaw open in confusion. One guy, a bit older than the rest and obviously unaware that his hip, horizontal-striped shirt did very little to hide that fact, adjusted a pair of glasses atop the wide bridge of his nose. Next to him stood a dark-haired woman in tight black clothing, arms exposed—one bare, one tatted from shoulder to wrist.

"You folks are out here in the dark without flashlights?" Grey asked.

The tallest member answered, "Why would we bring flashlights? We have a light on our camera."

"You look like you've lost a lot of blood," the guy with the glasses said. "We need to get you some medical attention."

Ignoring how little sense it made to rely on a camera for light, Grey looked down at his chest. Still moist except for the top corner, which had dried up. It was, in fact, very deep and very wide. "Oh shit. That doesn't look good."

"What happened to you?" the older guy with glasses said.

"Okay, this is gonna sound nuts, but there was this ... thing back there. This, like, woman in a nightgown or something. She had wings and claws and shit."

"Lady Hyne?" Glasses said. "You saw her?"

"Bullshit," Cheek Bones rebutted.

"Lady what? You know who I'm talking about? I didn't just see her, I think I might've ... killed her."

"He's a plant, dude!" Cheek Bones exclaimed.

"Johnson," the woman with the arm sleeve barked, "would you shut your damn mouth for just one second?"

Wait ... Johnson?

"You know Hope Hollow has a bunch of these people just perpetuating the myth to drive up tourism, right?!" Cheek Bones—Johnson—said.

Hold up ... Hope Hollow?

"Where are we?" Grey asked.

"The woods," Johnson replied.

"Oh, really?" Grey said sarcastically.

"Hope Hollow," Glasses answered.

Grey's mouth hung open, barely able to register a response. "... What?"

Glasses continued. "We're a documentary crew investigating the local legend of the Hope Hollow Witch."

Those glasses ...

That dumb striped shirt ...

Grey let out a confused breath.

It all clicked into place. The familiarity of the group before him—spitting images of the actors he'd just seen on-screen.

The old man at the pawn shop and his half-assed warning.

The bearded guy with the hoodie and his *full*-assed warning.

Whoever uses this camera becomes the subject of their own film.

Grey pointed at the guy with the glasses. "Larry?"

Larry gave him an odd look. "How do you ..."

Grey's finger hovered over to: "Caleb? ... Blaire?"

Each member of the group exchanged looks.

"Who the hell are you, man?" Johnson asked.

Grey put his hands on his head, scraping at his scalp and clinging on to whatever piece of sanity still remained inside of it. Looking back on his encounter with the bird woman, whom Larry had reverentially referred to as "Lady Hyne", Grey recalled her janky movements, the digitized wings that appeared to be animated, almost separate from her body, with the moonlight bouncing off of them unconvincingly. He was under too much duress at the time to take it for what it was:

Subpar visual effects in a low-budget movie.

His vision blurred, then sprouted black spots. His knees weakened.

"Shit ... I'm trapped in a goddamn found footage film."

THE ESCAPE

GREY AWAKENED WITH A stiff mattress against his back and a view of wooden boards above him. As his vision came into focus, it became clear that he was on the bottom unit of a bunk bed. A hall light beyond the door frame lit the contents of the room surrounding him—two suitcases, a nightstand with a digital clock next to the bunk beds, and a wooden dresser on the other end.

"We should have taken him to a hospital," a voice said from the other end of the hallway.

That sounded like Blaire, he thought.

The rest of the group chimed in as well.

"Come on," Johnson said, "we've all thought it, but no one wants to say it. This documentary could be a huge bust. What if all this Hope Hollow Witch stuff turns out to be a hoax? We have a new angle with this guy. What does this kind of cryptid myth mumbo jumbo do to the minds of the people living in an otherwise abandoned American town?"

Grey ran his fingertips over the bandage on his chest and winced at the tenderness of his stitched-together flesh.

"I can't believe I'm saying this," Larry responded, "but I agree with Johnson."

Grey rose from the bed, careful not to bump his head on the bunk above him. Damn, everything *hurt.* He swung his legs to the edge of the bed, groaning from the sharp pain in his chest and trying to understand the logistics of his predicament. Here he was, trapped in a make-believe world, but with every sense fully intact. He could bleed. He could get fatigued. He could be phsycially transported by a group of NPCs.

"Do we even know if it's safe to keep him around?" Caleb asked. "The guy's obviously a little ..."

"Nutso, right?" Johnson finished for him.

Grey rose from the bed and willed himself toward the conversation.

He got to the door frame as Caleb continued: "Unwell, I was gonna say. Did you hear the guy tell us he thinks he's in a movie? We're supposed to believe he went and slayed some flying demon?"

Their perspective on him didn't matter. All he cared about was finding his way out of this world and back into the theater. The documentary crew wasn't real—at least outside of this vacuum Grey found himself in. Within it, Grey had the good sense to know that his encounter with the bird-woman wasn't meant for him, and, as these things go in horror movies, that encounter was probably meant to go differently. Meant for someone else.

"Lady Hyne," Larry corrected, his voice becoming louder as Grey made his way through the hall.

"Who gives a shit what the make-believe monster lady's name is?" Johnson shot back. "The guy's probably just some town drunk who's heard one too many bedtime stories."

Screw it. Whatever was going on here, he could chalk it up to a bad fever dream. A glitch in the matrix. A ripple in space and time. The most important thing for Grey at this very moment was getting the hell out of Hope Hollow and getting back home.

Grey's footsteps were heavy enough, and he wondered when they'd realize he was creeping through the hallway, inching closer to the front door ...

"Do you guys hear that?" Johnson asked, providing Grey with an answer.

A thin table sat under a circular mirror at the far end of the hallway, and on that table was a set of keys. The largest key, the one Grey assumed was for the van, pointed to the front door across the hallway from it, practically begging him to snatch it up.

Grey Carter: Car thief in a make-believe world.

Did that make him a make-believe car thief?

With no subtle way of going about things, Grey grabbed the keys off the table and darted toward the front door, causing a series of *clacks* and *jingles* that effectively ruined his stealthy escape.

"Hey!" Johnson yelled.

But Grey was already out the door.

By the time he leapt inside the van, the documentary crew was outside the house as well.

Johnson leapt off the porch, yelling, "You get out of that van! Right now!" He sprinted to the van and slapped the driver's side window.

Grey cranked the engine and reversed, sending bursts of gravel and dust up into the glow of the headlights.

Which way had they pulled into the driveway in the movie? Left? Right?

Shit ... He didn't even make it that far in the movie.

So he guessed and turned left, steering the van into the dark mouth of the road, lined by two rows of bowing, crooked trees that seemed to be closing in on him the farther he went.

THE VOID

IT TOOK GREY SEVEN minutes to realize that everything had gone black.

Not black in terms of darkness. A deep, deep void left in the absence of color.

He'd driven straight into a great big nothing, the headlights showing his way forward in a floating car, dangling upright like a rocket in the vast vacuum of space. The tree limbs had merged with the sky. The sky had merged with the edge of the road.

The only thing that physically existed now was Grey and the van he was driving.

Grey put his foot on the brake, and the van slowed without a ground for the wheels to tread on. He stepped out, pressing his feet against an invisible surface, inhabiting a darkness so deep he could barely see his hands. Behind him, the world of the film was merely a speck of light, a minuscule promise of life at the other side of whatever *this* was.

A dread crept into his stomach, into his chest—a feeling that he knew to be true, but hated admitting. His existence was fleeting and insignificant. Even in this fake world, he couldn't escape the feeling of simply existing. Floating in suspended space. Yelling into a void that wouldn't respond.

The space, the infinite darkness of it all, welcomed his most somber thoughts. He couldn't be that person people needed him to be—

Stop.

Not Cassandra—

Stop!

Not little Michael—

Stop!

He belonged to an endless darkness that he couldn't pull himself free from, for he himself was the void.

"Hello?" a voice echoed from a direction Grey couldn't pinpoint.

"That sound ..." A voice again. This with a slow, painful drag as if sliding over glass. "Is that someone new?"

Grey spun aimlessly, scanning across a carousel of: Van, darkness, van, darkness.

"Take us to your world," another voice said. This one was closer ...

Behind him.

A damp hand touched his shoulder, its residue dripping down his shoulder. He jolted forward, pulling himself free and patting the sticky substance away. His hands peeled a sticky, tar-like substance.

He leapt into the van and pulled the door shut.

Automatic locks? ...

No such luck.

He locked the driver's side door manually, then turned to reach over to the passenger's side—

"Shit!" Grey screamed.

"Hi." A man with blackened skin and a long, fraying beard sat in the passenger's seat next to him, his eyes milky and grey like an old dog. He was all bones and no meat, with skin sunken down into his eye sockets, his entire skull protruding as if mistakenly placed on a smaller body.

The emaciated man strained to speak. "Fancy seeing you here."

A hand banged on Grey's window, causing him to jump again, and the realization that he was now smack dab in the middle of two unknowable threats stabbed at his chest like a power drill. Then another hand—and another and another—pounded against the windows of the van.

At least there was only *one* inside.

"Look," Grey said, somehow thinking that reasoning with the thing next to him would make his troubles disappear, "I'm not even supposed to be here. I don't know how I got to this place, man. I'm just trying to find my way back home."

The black, skeletal man shrugged. "I tried to warn you. If you'd paid attention, you'd know exactly why the fuck you're here."

"You ... what?" That beard. Those eyes. Sure, they were faded now, but they had a hint of that same greenish tint.

The vagabond.

"Holy shit," Grey muttered as the car continued to rock, "You're that guy."

That guy nodded.

"What the hell is going on?" Greg asked.

"I had the camera before you did, brother. Whatever the hell it is, the thing wants to be entertained. I've had a lot of time to think. Not much else to do out here, if you can believe it." He chuckled, giving his lungs a workout they couldn't manage, and they coughed in protest. "Least I haven't been out in the void as long as these folks have." He waved his finger ahead.

Trapped in the headlights were walking corpses, dripping with the black and browning rot of their own skin, their lips receding into their gums. Their faces were merely skulls with yellow teeth and milky orbs for eyes.

"What are they?" Grey asked.

"My theory? Poor souls who didn't finish their story. Either the camera consumes the story, or it consumes a piece of you. I didn't finish it. I failed. Eventually, I'll be like them, I think. I hope my mind goes before the rest of me."

"But I just saw you out in the real world."

"Ah, see? I said it consumes a *piece* of you. My brain's scrambled now. Split between this place and the real world. Twenty-four hours a day spent in the light and in the dark, all at the same time. It's enough to break a man down. And I was already broken to begin with."

The metal of the van's exterior rattled viciously in Grey's ear. He knew he had to leave fast, but, against his better instincts, he took a moment and told the man, "I'm sorry."

The man attempted to smile, raising a cheek and causing his upper lip the crack. "Last decent thing I can do is guide you on your way. Go finish the story. Complete the film."

Grey had never seen someone this utterly defeated. A deflated balloon of a human simply sinking into the fabric of a car seat. Sinking into a sandpit of misery and hopelessness, having lost the energy to even care about it.

The brass of Michael's compass nestled in Grey's pocket poked at his thigh more prominently now. A reminder of the world waiting for him on the other side.

Screw it.

Grey put the van in reverse. "Why don't we do it together, man? I'm takin' you with me."

"Doesn't work like that, compadre. Those things out there have been around so long they forgot. We all got our own stories to fix. Can't live in someone else's reality."

Grey ignored him and stomped on the gas pedal, rumbling over bony bodies as he slid backward toward his new reality. It wasn't just that he felt sorry for the man; Grey was scared. Scared that he would end up the same way—a collection of bones with his life and memories fading off of his very frame. With this man—whatever his name was—at his side, someone who'd failed before him, he might have a leg up. He might be able to beat this thing and get back home. Might be able to avoid the same mistakes.

The stumbling corpses faded from existence until there was nothing beyond the headlights. That speck of unreality grew larger in the rearview mirror—the charcoal of the street, that navy blue sky, the moonlight.

"Let's do this thing," Grey said.

When he looked to his right, the vagabond was gone.

Grey looked back behind his headrest, catching two rows of seats and no malnourished zombie corpse.

The man had left behind a palpable sadness in his wake, something thick and dreadful, hopeless, even. It was the kind of sadness Grey had become reluctant friends with. The type that made him want to scream. And whenever he wanted to scream, he smiled instead, because smiling was easier than explaining why he wanted to scream.

He kept his foot on the pedal, finally breaking free of the void and re-entering Hope Hollow.

He slowed, making sure to get a solid look at the black hole and the edge that surrounded it.

In that moment, the only thing he wished for was to fill that space with color.

He wished to immerse himself in the living room he'd walked out of earlier that day. To be in the presence of his sister and nephew.

Complete the film, the words of the vagabond reminded him.

And that's what the—

—*fudge*—

—he would do.

THE RETURN

GETTING BACK TO THE documentary crew's cabin was a straight shot. There wasn't much real estate in Hope Hollow, and Grey remembered well enough how the cabin looked in the daylight just based on the first ten minutes of the movie.

The movie ... Dang. Some time ago—maybe two hours if he had to guess—he was sitting in an empty movie theater slap-fighting with an employee. A stalled "career", few actual friends, very little money. And now, he'd do anything to park his keister in one of those red-cushioned theater seats. The ones with the vague stains on them that—*Yikes*—he hoped were only from soda and butter.

When he pulled the car into the gravel driveway of the cabin, Johnson was on the stoop looming like a tall shadow with the porch light at his back. He marched down the steps to meet Grey as the front door opened and the rest of the crew peeked out.

"Well, if it isn't sleeping beauty himself!" Johnson yelled.

"Is that supposed to be an insult?" Grey half responded, half said to himself. Johnson wouldn't have heard it over the engine anyway.

"Careful, Johnson! He's injured!" Blaire called out from the stoop.

"Yeah, and he's about to be even *more* injured when I'm through pounding his face in." Johnson slapped the hood of the car. "Get out, buttercup!"

Grey killed the engine. "Not exactly top-notch dialogue here, guys." He could only assume Johnson was supposed to die early. His humor wasn't the witty comic relief type; it was the insufferable moron type. Cannon fodder for a shocking kill.

Grey cut off the engine, then opened the driver's side door and stepped out. "I come in peace, Mr. Johnson." Grey spoke loud enough to address the entire group. "And I'm sorry I stole your van. A lot of freaky things have happened in the past, uh ... however many hours it's been."

Blaire stepped down from the porch, breaking away from the rest of the crew huddled by the door. "You should be resting," Blaire said.

"This guy drives off with our van and your response is, 'You should be resting?!'" Johnson yelled. "Where were you even going, guy? And what were you doing in those woods? You were spouting off pure nonsense when he found you."

Grey walked past Johnson and Blair, closing the distance between them and the porch where Caleb and Larry stood. "Thanks for patching me up. I'm still figuring out how things work here, but I know that I'd be in bad shape if it weren't for you all. Honestly, though, you might want to thank me too."

"Why's that?" Larry asked.

"You guys were out here doing a bit of snooping, right?" Grey answered. "Someone was probably stupid enough to suggest you split up?"

Caleb tilted his head. "I was going to suggest it, actually. I brought an extra camera in my bag, just in case."

"Ah," Grey responded. "So after you all split up, one of you might've encountered that bird thing that I stumbled upon. Who knows what might've happened then, ya know?"

"I would have smashed its beak in," Johnson said. "That is, if what you said is even true."

Larry stepped down from the porch. "We have a lot of questions for you. For one, how did you know our names?"

"Oh, uh ..." *Think fast.* "I overheard you guys before you found me. You know you address each other by name, like ... pretty regularly."

"I don't think we do," Larry replied.

"Well ... there's no logical explanation besides that, is there?"

Larry's eyes tilted up before landing on Grey again. "No, I guess not."

"Give us one reason why we should trust you," Johnson said. "Are you just some weird towny looking to exploit us? Not much to do here, and you just want to mess with the out-of-towners, right?"

That sparked an idea, and Grey had to turn it into a good pitch. After all, this group *was* the subject of the film, and, therefore, his only hope of getting out of this situation and back to his normal life. His only hope at fixing things.

He didn't know anything about the Hope Hollow Witch ... But he *did* know a thing or two about found footage movies.

"Ah, wait ... My head's all fuzzy." Grey grabbed the sides of his head and grimaced, really making a show of his phony headache. "I've felt so confused."

"Some trauma to the head, maybe?" Blaire asked.

Thank you, Blaire.

"Yes," Grey replied. "That must've been why my memory's all shot. I'm sorry for stealing your van. I've been so disoriented. Things are starting to come back to me now ... I was out there looking for the Witch. What I got instead was that little dick-head minion."

"Why were you out there looking for it?" Caleb asked.

"Yeah, just for funzies?" Johnson added.

Think fast, Grey thought again. "Because ..." *Come on!* "... my sister got lost in the woods here. Went on a ... camping trip at Hope Hollow?" It came out like a question, forcing Grey to compose himself. "And she was, you know, never seen again."

"Oh no," Blaire whispered, an expression of real sympathy, something that lodged a knife of guilt in Grey's stomach.

"You want to catch this witch on camera?" Grey asked. "I'm your best shot. And you want a good documentary? I can help you. I'm the only one here who's gone toe-to-toe with a lurker in the woods, so clearly I have a nose for this stuff."

Channel Bruce Willis in Armageddon, Grey thought, gritting his teeth. "I *will* find the Hope Hollow Witch ... I swear to God I will."

"We're gonna need to see some proof first," Caleb objected. "Bunch of people claim to see Bigfoot, but no one seems to get one on camera."

"Then let's go get some proof," Grey shot back.

"You wanna go *back out* there?" Blaire asked.

Larry stepped forward. "He's right. It's the only way we can tell if this guy's for real or not. If you can take us to the body ... consider yourself a part of the crew. Not everyone has to go."

"No," Blaire retorted, "We're sticking together."

Smart woman, Grey thought. His money was on Blaire making it to the end.

Grey asked the group, "Anybody have a weapon?"

THE BUY-IN

GREY WALKED IN THE middle of the group as they traced their steps back to the spot at which they'd found him. Caleb led the way with his camera light beaming, powered by never-ending battery life. He chatted with a fire-poker-wielding Johnson as they shot poorly-concealed insults back and forth.

"Are we really gonna let him inside?" "We already did." "The guy's obviously nuts, right?" "If things go south, at the very least, we have a local fanatic to give us a spin on local myths and hysteria and shit." That last one, of course, was Johnson.

"Here," Blaire said from his side, handing Grey a water bottle. "You must be thirsty."

Yes, he *was* thirsty.

Grey craned his neck, looking between her and Larry, thinking that Blaire was exactly the type of girl he'd swipe right on in the real world. He might've taken his shot, but the opening of the film clearly established that Blaire and Larry had a thing, and Grey needed to shepherd that relationship to fruition if it was a part of the overall arc.

Grey took the bottle. "Thank you." Grey chugged, gulping embarrassingly loud in the sudden quiet.

"Apparently you think you're in a movie, huh?" Johnson asked. "What's *that* shit all about?"

Grey's eyes shifted down. "I had a camera in my face, so ... yeah, I thought I was in a movie."

"A found footage movie, you said?" Larry asked.

Grey took another sip from the water bottle, finishing it, and wiped a drop from his chin. "You don't know what that is?"

No one answered.

"*Blair Witch Project*? *Paranormal Activity*? *Cloverfield*? *Cannibal Holocaust*? ... No?" Grey could have kept going.

Still, he was met with silence.

"What, are those really obscure titles?" Larry asked. "Video nasties or something? I know a lot about film history, and I've never heard of those."

Grey laughed lightly to himself, because, sure, why *would* they know any of those titles? "Listen, like I said before, I was really disoriented. You know, because of the head trauma and all. Just a little out of sorts."

Caleb called out to the group, "If I remember correctly, this was right around the spot where we found you."

Grey eyed the spot where he collapsed, focusing on the thick branch hanging at eye level that had taken his brain on a joy ride. He walked toward the branch and stared into the vanishing abyss of leaves and tree limbs beyond it. "I ran in from that direction. Must've been running forrrrr two minutes, maybe? We don't have long to go." He eyed the iron rod at Johnson's side, the dull notch facing outward at the end of it. "Might wanna be prepared to use that thing."

Grey was as frightened as any guy walking in the woods at night could be, but he'd already killed the thing they were headed toward, and he liked the odds of that being the only monster in the woods tonight.

Could he die here?

He could certainly bleed.

Get back to Michael, he reminded himself.

They paced through the woods with Grey in front, his outline casting a black, elongated replica on the earth in front of him, outlined by the light of Caleb's camera that he wasn't blocking.

"No way," Caleb said as he aimed the light at a bloodied tree branch lodged into the ground. Bits of gut hung along the sides, topped off by a large intestine dangling from the high end.

It wasn't the image Grey had hoped to stumble upon. Not quite the evidence that would have converted them from skeptics to true believers. But it was *something* at the very least.

"Come on, guys," Johnson said. "This could have been from anything. A wild boar. A bear. A deer."

Caleb scanned the wide, bloody line trailing off from the limb—probably blowing his entire wad at the footage he was capturing, Grey figured.

"Go back to the base of that tree limb," Larry commanded.

Caleb did, focusing in on the dirt surrounding the jagged wooden spike.

"Look at the scratch marks," Larry said. And indeed, the dirt around the base was dug up in wide scars. About five feet away, the marks were thinner. Sharper. Vicious. "Two areas of digging. One looks like hands made it. The other ... claws."

"Bullshit," Johnson said. "I don't buy it."

"I can't be the only one freaked out by this, right?" Blaire said. "Whatever got impaled just, what? Got up and walked away? It could still be out here. Seems like a good time to gun it back to H.Q., doesn't it?"

"Or maybe another animal ate it," Johnson said plainly.

"Uh ... I'm with Blaire," Caleb said, scanning the ground with his camera. "These are definitely ..."

Captured in the light, a series of three-pronged, red tracks formed a path.

They were unmistakably the tracks of a large bird.

"Footprints," Grey said.

"Let's get the hell out of the woods," Blaire said.

"Wait," Grey said, his zoning in on whatever features he could make out beyond Caleb's light. He walked forward, craning his neck and questioning his memory—and perhaps his sanity. Where there had been a clearing, there were now trees, and the stone structure that the bird woman had perched on top of was gone. Swallowed into the earth.

"There was a building here," Grey said. "This was all different when I was ..."

"A building?" Larry repeated. "What do you mean? What did it look like?"

"Made of stone. All these vines growing on it. Something that the Crypt Keeper might've lived in," Grey answered, quickly realizing how much crazier he was sounding with each passing syllable. "You know what, I think I'm misremembering. I'm a little foggy."

Johnson scoffed. "Oh, look at that. He's a little foggy."

But Larry gave Grey a knowing look. A look that told Grey that something had clicked into place. Grey had found the believer in the group. He'd earned Larry's trust.

"Blaire's right. We should get back to the cabin," Larry said. "There was definitely *something* here. It might not be safe for us to be in the woods right now."

As the whole crew turned to leave the site, a piece of silver fabric shimmered in Caleb's camera light—a momentary glare that disappeared as quickly as it had sparkled.

"Hold up," Grey said. "Caleb, let me get some light over here."

Johnson, predictably, said, "We don't take orders from you, pal—"

"Johnson, dude, could you please just..." Grey's Johnson-patience meter was already on empty. Johnson was so infuriatingly annoying and testosterone-fueled that Grey knew he was destined to be cannon fodder soon. Grey wouldn't facilitate it, but he wasn't sure if he'd mourn it either ...

Caleb turned the light back over to Grey, and the same object twinkled like an ornament on a Christmas tree. Grey walked closer to it, careful not to block Caleb's light.

It was something silver with black at the ends, splayed out on the ground like a flattened shirt.

But it wasn't a shirt.

It was a gaudy, sparkly, silver vest.

Rodney, Grey thought. *He's in here too.*

Next to the vest, etched haphazardly in the dirt, were a series of letters that spelled out:

THE WITCH LIVES

The scene felt eerily like a display, as if whoever had curated it *wanted* it to be discovered.

"Rodney!" he shouted.

He was quickly shushed by Johnson, who grabbed his shoulder simultaneously.

"Are you nuts?" Johnson said. "We need to go, *now*."

THE GAMEPLAN

THEY'D HUSTLED QUICKLY BACK toward the house, not a single one of them failing to glance back over their shoulders or jump at the snap of a twig. Grey knew any wooded area to be alive at night with creatures and critters lurking and debris falling. But the crew had just seen his story validated—at least in part—and it spooked the heck out of them.

Even Johnson, who only looked back once and played it off, his face contorting from concerned to mean mugging at Grey as if he were cycling through emotions in an acting class.

It was strange for Grey to be in the living room that he'd just seen on screen, the same one he'd watched the camera drift through, with its uber-modern, yet cozy aesthetic. The leather chair, probably well over a thousand bucks if he had to guess, was a welcome relief for his legs, which were already beginning to stiffen as the lactic acid set in. That sprint away from the bird woman was the most he'd run in weeks, and if he got out of this place—*when* he got out of this place—he'd make sure to change that.

They settled in around the coffee table. Johnson placed himself on the couch, Caleb sat in the adjacent leather chair, staring into the viewfinder of his camera as it recorded, and Larry flipped the switch next to the fireplace, kickstarting the flame.

When Blaire came to Grey with another bottle of water, he realized how dry his mouth was, how much he'd been neglecting his hydration. But Blaire was on top of it for him, nurturing him in a way he'd never experienced before.

"Where's *my* water?" Johnson asked as Blaire sat next to him on the couch.

"In the faucet," she answered with her eyes trained on Grey. "That name you shouted in the woods. Rodney. Who is that?"

"Uh ..." Another lie incoming. He couldn't say he'd travelled here with the man formerly known as Rodney, could he? That would lead to too many questions. "Just a guy in town who agreed to take me places others wouldn't. Kinda like a tour guide. We got separated when that bird demon thing attacked us. I ... I hope he's okay." Grey genuinely meant in. Though it had been Rodney whose actions had somehow set off the camera, it was ultimately Grey who was responsible for them being there. He was the one who'd smuggled a cursed camera into the theater after Rodney had told him not to.

From the kitchen sink, Johnson said, "Don't expect us to send out a search party, bud."

Rodney's words replayed in Grey's head. *I've seen it. A few times, actually*. Between those words and the ominous note etched in mud, Grey wondered if Rodney may have stumbled into his element.

He'd somehow manage to find Rodney and bring him back, but for now, Grey would have to play the role he'd created for himself.

"If he knows the woods, I'm sure he can take care of himself," Blaire said. "At least ... I hope he can." She sighed. "What do you know about this bird demon thing?"

"Lady Hyne," Larry interjected, standing by the fireplace with his arms crossed.

"Yep, what he said," Grey agreed.

Larry continued. "According to legend, in the 1700s, certain groups in these parts were seen as royalty. They experimented with witchcraft to see if they could create a superior race, and the Witch of Hope Hollow was their primary consultant."

"They weren't burning witches back then?" Blaire asked.

"Not everywhere," Larry replied. "Where some places saw rampant superstition, others saw opportunity. The royal class of Hope Hollow attempted to instill supernatural abilities within their offspring. Some of the children manifested genetic abnormalities. Lady Hyne was one such case."

"Jesus," Blaire said.

"I don't think Jesus has much of a place in Hope Hollow," Larry replied.

Oo that's a good line, Grey thought.

"Did I get all that right, Grey?" Larry asked.

"Huh?" Grey squirmed in his seat. "Oh, yeah. Couldn't have said it any better myself."

"What did she look like?" Blaire asked.

"An absolute nightmare," Grey responded. "Her lips were sewn shut, and she had these massive, veiny eyes popping out of her skull."

Larry nodded. "According to legend, the villagers sewed her mouth shut when she began cursing the children. She couldn't have a normal childhood, so why should everyone else, right?"

He crouched down, lowering his eyeline to Grey. "Did you really see her?"

Grey didn't know what else he could have said at that point to buy their trust, so he slipped into the role he'd created for himself. "I'd been tracking it—her—all week. Just got a little too close for comfort. I'm lucky I didn't come away with a curse on me."

"Bullshit," Johnson said, rejoining the group with a glass of water.

"We have an extra bed you can stay in," Larry said, rising back up.

"Dude ..." Johnson said.

Caleb looked up from his viewfinder. "I have a toothbrush he can borrow."

"Bro ..." Johnson shot back.

"We follow the schedule," Larry commanded. "Tomorrow, we go out for some on-the-street-style interviews. Get the locals' perspectives on the legend."

Johnson pointed an accusatory finger at Grey. "I'm not sleeping near this guy. We still don't know if we can trust him."

"I'll sleep in the van, then," Grey said. "Lock the doors. Just give me some blankets and some water, and I'll be fine."

The crew looked among each other, understanding it was probably for the best. It didn't matter to Grey. The van had withstood a beating from the decrepit former-humans in the void. Besides, he'd changed the film. Things were different now. This was a game he could play and win. An opponent whose moves he could anticipate. The next run-in wouldn't be an attack—no, it would be a bad omen.

A promise of things to come.

THE BAD OMEN

"IT'S NOT THE RITZ, but it'll do," Grey said while staring into the interior of the van. The backseat folded down into a bed, and, while it wasn't ideal, it wasn't the worst surface he'd ever slept on. Larry had helped him pack in the blankets from whatever beds weren't occupied inside the house, which he hoped would help to soften the brick-like seat cushions.

"I just don't want you to freeze out here," Larry said. "You know, you really don't have to—"

"Hey, if it makes you feel any better, just chalk it up to this being my preference. I *want* to sleep in the van. Look at this thing. Plus, I don't have the keys, so there's no way for me to drive away."

Larry laughed. "That thing about your sister ... I'm really sorry. I actually lost my sister last year as well. Well ... lost as in she went missing. Absentia is what they call it. Once people have been lost long enough, people just rule out that they might still be alive."

Grey's heart rate quickened. Knowingly or not, he'd jacked this guy's storyline. And as nervous as that made him, his split-second decision to invoke the lost sibling trope might've been the thing keeping him here. Larry had lost someone for real, and thus may have felt a kinship of sorts with Grey.

"I'm so sorry to hear that," Grey said. "Maybe she's ..." He didn't finish. What was the right thing to say? Was hope just a cruel fixation in the face of Larry's loss?

"Still out there?" Larry chuckled. "That's what people say. As a filmmaker, I don't rule anything out. Just like you shouldn't rule out your sister still being out in those woods somewhere."

Grey nodded, not knowing what else to say.

"I need you to look me in the eye, Grey," Larry said, his eyes forming a straight line through Grey's retina. "I need you to tell me you really saw that stone house."

The eye contact made Grey uncomfortable, but this wasn't a lie he needed to keep. He knew what he saw, and any internal bullshit detector Larry was utilizing would come back negative.

"I saw that house," Grey said. "It was out there. It's not anymore, and I can't explain it. Just like I can't explain the woman with wings."

Larry held his gaze for an uncomfortably long time, irises jutting outward.

Finally, Larry said, "Welcome to the team."

Grey slid open the van door in the morning, letting the sunlight warm his body. Before he took his first step out of the van, an object halted his progress.

Sitting in the gravel driveway right at the point that his feet would have landed was a figure made of twigs with hair jutting out from the top of it.

Grey stepped down and leaned over the object. The hardened mane atop the stick sculpture was real. Whether from a human or an animal, he couldn't tell.

THE MOVIE MAGIC

JOHNSON WAS THE LAST to step out of the van. "Thank God. It smelled like ass in there."

It didn't smell like ass. The rest of the crew had begun to ignore Johnson more frequently.

The ride into town had been dominated by speculation about the stick figure that was placed next to the van.

Could it have been the townsfolk messing with them?

Maybe.

Lady Hyne or even the Hope Hollow Witch dropping off a trinket to foreshadow their demise?

Also likely.

But Larry, the inquisitive documentarian, was unfamiliar with the offering and had to think someone in town would know what it meant.

The gas station had just two pumps, and the sign above the convenience store wasn't any kind of oil provider Grey was familiar with. Two men sat beside each other, sinking into lawn chairs next to the ice cooler, their skin cracked and dry like leather. Larry had spotted them first and decided they'd be perfect for a run-and-gun interview.

Larry approached first with a big smile. Caleb trailed behind him with the camera, and Blaire with a shotgun mic and headphones. That put Grey and Johnson on the same relative playing field—useless to the construction of the documentary.

"So you're the producer, huh?" Grey asked Johnson as Larry buttered up the locals in the distance.

Johnson gave him a suspicious look. "I didn't tell you that. How'd you know?"

"You and I are the only ones without equipment. And Larry is definitely the director. Every movie needs a producer."

Johnson shrugged, uninterested in keeping the conversation going. "Yep, I'm the money guy."

"No, you don't just manage the money. I mean, that's what everyone probably thinks, right?"

Johnson perked up, his face softening as Grey continued. "You handle logistics. Permits if needed. Scheduling. Interviews. You oversee the whole project, right? It's a big job."

"Yeah ... it is." Johnson's eyebrows furrowed in confusion. It may have been the only time someone had taken him seriously since they'd started their trip.

"We're on!" Larry hollered back to the crew.

Time to make some movie magic happen.

The Witch of Hope Hollow
Timecode: 18:44:56

Two men in lawn chairs appear in the frame, sitting in front of a gas station. Their skin is damaged by years of sun exposure. Each of them could be a haggard fifty-five or a tired sixty-six. It's difficult to tell. Neither of them seems to be incredibly enthusiastic about being interviewed.

Local #1 has a bushy white beard and speaks through a wad of chewing tobacco.

Local #2 wears a frayed hat with an embroidered fish above the brim.

The camera zooms in on a spray painted message above their heads on the side of the gas station that reads, "THE WITCH LIVES." It zooms back out to capture the locals in frame.

Local #1 says, "Most people here just try to keep to themselves. This Hope

Hollow Witch stuff, maybe it's real, maybe it's not. Nobody I know is dumb enough to go snoopin' around to find out."

Local #2 adds, "Lots of people 'round these parts claim they've seen either the Witch or her acolytes. Hunters and people who go campin' out in the woods.

Off-screen, Larry asks, "You mentioned her acolytes. What can you tell us about that?"

"Well," Local #2 says, "people say she apparently has a small group of cursed folk who go around and do her bidding."

"Do her bidding?" Local #1 repeats. "What the hell does that mean?"

"Hell, I don't know," Local #2 says. "I'm just tellin' 'em what people done told me is all."

Larry jumps in, trying to get the interview back on the rails. "Do you know the names of any of these acolytes off the top of your heads?"

Local #2 takes a long, deep breath. "Weeeelllllll, there's this bird-human hybrid called Lady Hyne. Then there's the Butcher Farrow. He got a spike for a hand. A machete 'r somethin'? Oh, and Willie Longlegs. He got limbs that bend the wrong way, so he crawls around like a spider."

Local #1 grunts. "Folks just blowin' smoke, y'all."

"My second cousin says she seen Willie Longlegs!" Local #2 says.

"That the cousin who done smoked enough crack to incapacitate a damn gorilla?"

"You know good and goddamn well Darla don't smoke that shit! She—"

CUT TO

A man in a three-piece suit sits behind a wooden desk. A collage of various framed accolades—degrees, certifications—lines the wall behind him.

"My buddy was the mayor for a time," the man says, "and I kept tellin' him we needed to milk this Hope Hollow Witch thing for profit. Make this a tourist attraction. Kinda like how Roswell's got little Area 51 pop-up shops. He never saw the value in it."

Off-screen, Larry says, "But you do get tourists out here looking for proof of the Witch, correct?"

"Oh, yessir, we do," Local #3 says. "I try to mind my own business with them, though. It's one thing to come as a tourist and delve into the history of this place, but if you go lookin' for the Witch …" The man shakes his head slowly.

"How do you mean?" Larry asks.

Local #3 shrugs. "Rumor has it that the Witch has this machine that uses ancient technology and magic. Lures in the curious ones. People like you folks who would be silly enough to seek her out. Sacrifices them and loads their souls up into this magic machine to give her life and bring her into the real world. That's why … lotta people don't end up comin' back."

The man pauses with a stern look on his face …

Before melting into a laugh.

"Was that good?" he asks. "Y'all gonna use that for the movie?"

The crew behind the camera laughs.

"Oh, we're definitely gonna use it," Larry says.

In an instant, like someone remote-piloting the man in the three-piece suit pushed a button, the man switches from a laugh to a stern look again. "Don't go lookin' for that witch, though … Seriously."

The group behind the camera goes silent.

"Um … okay. Noted," Larry says.

CUT TO

A man wearing overalls and sitting in his truck says, "Hope Hollow Witch? Yeah, I've had a direct encounter with her. She slept with my best friend, then tried to get alimony from me. We talkin' bout the same person, right? My ex-wife?"

He laughs.

CUT TO

A woman in a button-down blouse and fitted jeans stands next to a moving truck with the back wide open. Stacked boxes fill the inside of the truck cabin.

"A documentary? Local legend type stuff?" the woman asks.

"Yes, ma'am," Larry says from behind the camera.

"You all look pretty young. Is this for a school project?" There's genuine curiosity in her question. Maybe even a hint of adoration.

"Actually, it is," Larry says. "I'm a professor and these here are students on an internship getting some real-world experience."

"Oh, wow, that's really cool." She smiles. "I'm not from around here, so I'm not sure how much help I'll be. I'm just helping my mom move."

Larry replies, "That's perfectly fine. Could you just repeat what you just said about the Hope Hollow Witch right before we started recording?"

The woman straightens up. "Yeah, my mom told me she saw the Hope Hollow Witch once. Well … she heard her in the woods stomping around while she and her friends were out camping."

"Any chance we might be able to speak with her?" Larry asks.

"She's inside, but … she's dealing with a bit of dementia. It's not terrible—not *yet*, at least—but she's not exactly all there. I don't think she'd like anyone in the house."

Johnson says, "Ma'am, we'll be in and out in five minutes, tops. We just want to hear her story. This man to my right lost his sister to those woods, and any information your mother might be able to provide could help get her back."

The woman looks to the right of the frame. "Your sister's missing?"

Grey responds, "Uh … yeah. She's totally missing."

The woman sighs. "Alright … Five minutes."

CUT TO

The interior of the house is packed floor to ceiling with books and newspapers. A quick shot of the dining room reveals a large wood-and-glass cabinet with china stacked inside and stacks of hardbacks barricading the pristine plates behind the cabinet's glass.

The woman in the button-down blouse leads the crew into the living room. "As you can see, my mom's a bit of a packrat. It's too much even for the local thrift shop. I've spent all week trying to get rid of it."

An old woman with a haggard smoker's voice calls out. "Annabelle? Back so soon?"

Annabelle turns back, looking past the camera while continuing her walk into the living room. "I don't want our names to be in this. Is that okay?"

Larry's disembodied voice responds, "Of course."

Entering the living room, Anabelle approaches an elderly woman in a recliner, sitting with a blanket over her lap.

Annabelle crouches next to her. "Momma, these people here are making a movie."

The old woman stares glassy-eyed at her uninvited guests. "Oh, isn't that something?"

"They're hoping you can talk about your encounter with the Hope Hollow Witch, Momma," Annabelle says.

THE WARNING

"Ma'am, is there anything you can tell us about the night you went camping with your friends?" Larry asked.

"I don't much like talking about it," the old woman said.

"One of them lost their sister in the woods. They're just looking for any information that might help," Annabelle said.

The old woman looked up at the group, browsing each member with her eyes. "Oh, I'm so sorry about your sister."

Grey was really starting to feel self-conscious about this lie. Like he had a bomb strapped to his chest, and soon someone would find the button to detonate it.

"It's okay," Grey said. "I'm just looking to make sense of it."

"My friends and I should have never stayed in those woods. Things ain't been the same with us since."

"How do you mean?" Larry asked.

"That night changed us. We all came away marked. Poisoned. Ever since that night, I been hearin' these whispers. Not all the time. But for forty years, they come and go." The woman looked at her daughter. "You remember Dotty Jean, don't you?"

Annabelle looked downward, then looked at the crew. "Dotty Jean was her best friend. She, uh ... killed herself a couple years back."

"I never told you what she said to me on the phone before she did it, though. She said 'they', whoever they were, wanted her to *kill*. And she wasn't like that before. She would tell me about the glowing door. That's what she called it. The glowing door. She said that this voice that kept talkin' to her in her dreams, sometimes even when she was awake, told her to bring three children to the glowing door. Three souls for her three beautiful children."

"Did she ever ... act on that request?" Larry asked.

Annabelle had become increasingly uncomfortable, her face having sunken into a deep frown, her eyes hovering back and forth from her mother to Larry. The look told Grey that she was nearly ready to cut the interview off.

"Dotty told me she did," the old woman said.

"Did what exactly?" Larry pressed.

"She lured a couple of teenagers to that glowing door. Said that once you see the glowing door, it puts you in a trance. And that's when the Witch takes your soul. Kills you."

"Mom ..." Annabelle muttered.

"She couldn't go through with it. Snapped them out of the trance and scared them off."

"Do you know the names of these kids?" Larry asked.

Annabelle held up a hand. "I think we're done here."

"It's all because she took that damned offering home," the old woman said. "I know it."

"Offering?" Larry repeated.

"I wouldn't know what else to call it. She took it as a keepsake. When the whispers started, she tried to dispose of it, but it just kept coming back. She'd find it on the floor outside her bedroom door. On the windowsill gettin' rained on. It was this bundle of twigs and hair made to look like a tiny little figurine."

Grey's eyes widened as if forming the "oh" before "shit".

"Did it look a bit like this?" Johnson took the twig figure out of his pocket.

Though her eyes had faded, the old woman registered immediately what he was holding. She leaned forward in her chair, bearing what little teeth remained in her gums. "Get it away from me! Get out!"

"I'm sorry," Larry said. "We didn't mean to upset y—"

"Get the hell out of my house!" the old woman yelled. She pressed her hands against the armrests and kicked her heels into the footrest, forcing it back into the chair.

"Momma, don't," Annabelle said.

"You brought evil into this house!" the old woman yelled. "You're damned! All of you are damned!"

THE DINER

GREY AND BLAIRE SAT across from each other at the local diner. The window gave Grey a view of the parking lot, where Larry and Caleb were wrangling cables and equipment and getting Caleb's footage transferred to a hard drive.

The footage, admittedly, was pure gold.

"I think you're gonna have yourselves a good documentary," Grey said to Blaire as she scanned over the menu.

"I hope so," she said. "I graduate in a few months, and I only have a couple lame internships that aren't worth bragging about."

Her voice trembled. Grey snuck a glance at her hand as it gripped the menu a bit too tight. She was shaking.

An older, feminine voice snatched Grey's attention. "Where y'all comin' in from?"

Grey and Blaire turned their heads in unison. A woman in her fifties with frizzy hair—jet black to match her apron—and weathered skin approached their table with a steaming coffee pot. Grey welcomed the aroma as it wafted from the pot and under his nose. After a long morning trekking through the town, one cup just simply wouldn't do the trick.

"Do we stick out *that* much?" Blaire gave a knowing giggle. "Chicago."

"Ah, artsy city," the woman said.

"It is," Blaire responded.

"Y'all must be the ones makin' that movie about the local legend, huh?"

Blaire and Grey shared a glance.

"News travels fast, hon'," the woman said. "Some people here got a stick up their asses for that kind o' stuff, but truth is, tourism's good for Hope Hollow. Anyone gives you trouble, you come see Martha Mae." With her free hand, she pointed to her name tag, which did, in fact, read "Martha Mae".

"Thank you, Martha Mae," Grey said.

"Y'all look like you could use a slice of cranberry pie," Martha Mae said. "Folks say the Witch drives tourism here, but outta-towners come from far away to get a slice of my cranberry pie. First one's on the house, because, well ... you'll want a second and a third."

Grey caught a smirk from Blaire in his periphery and smiled. "A slice sounds great," he said.

With a nod and a wink, Martha Mae left the table and tended to the one behind them.

Grey leaned over to Blaire and said, "Good to see there's some nice folks here after the day we've had."

"Yeah." Blaire's smile faded quickly.

"You get a little spooked back there?" Grey asked.

Blaire laid the menu down flat. Took a breath. "It was fun, you know? The idea of us coming out here and chasing a little ghost story, making a spooky documentary about an urban legend. But now ... things just seem to be getting a little too real.

Whether there's a witch or not, *someone* left that trinket for us outside the house, right?"

"You think we've been ... marked?" Grey asked.

"I don't know. I just know that I've never been chased out of a house by a sexagenarian like that. Then, of course, there's your sister."

"What about her?"

"Well, she went missing in the woods. That makes all of this feel ... even more real. I'm sorry, by the way. I don't think I've said that yet."

"Oh, it's ... fine."

"No, it's not. I really am sorry. Could you tell me about her? If you don't mind."

Grey had to keep that switch in his brain flipped on. All he could think to do was call upon the real Cassandra, merge her with the construct he'd created on a whim. Give her a face, a personality, flesh.

"Cassandra. She's ... strong. Much stronger than me. In fact, she makes me feel like an infant trying to get my legs under me with how strong she is. Doesn't take any shit from anyone. She always has her shit together in a way I don't, I guess because she has to. She's raising a kid alone—" He'd gone too far with his merging experiment, leaving himself wide open for some very justifiable questions.

Questions which came out in a rapid-fire sequence. "Oh my god," Blaire said. "She has a child, and she's missing? How long has she been gone? Who's caring for the child?"

"Uh, a few months," Grey answered quickly. "As for who's taking care of Michael, uh, it's a family affair. My parents watch him mostly ..." *Wrong*. Their parents had been divorced for nine years and were on the other side of the country. "... and I help out as often as I can." That felt wrong as well. Grey had never been as involved as he could've been or needed to be, and here he was fabricating a bond between himself and Michael, putting it on a pedestal to perpetuate a facade.

Blaire put her hand on his. In a very literal sense, it was the type of warmth he hadn't experienced in years. With Blaire's palm against the back of Grey's hand, he realized she'd stopped shaking.

Lured into a state of vulnerability, Grey's hand acted faster than his brain as he reached down to his pocket and pulled out Michael's compass. He *wanted* to share more with Blaire. Maybe because she seemed to genuinely care.

"Michael gave this to me last time I saw him," Grey said. "He wants to join the Boy Scouts."

"You're a good brother and a good uncle," Blaire said. "I can tell. I really hope we can help you ..." She trailed off, perhaps wanting to finish the sentence with a positive notion that competed with the impossibility of the circumstances.

He picked up the thread and finished the thought for her. "Maybe I can at least find peace."

Real or not, the world Grey was now inhabiting had all of the familiar characteristics of reality. The smell of bacon grease on a fryer, the clanking of metal spatulas, the ambiance of chatter and commotion that gave this old-fashioned diner life. Outside of this metal structure, there was an entire world bursting with light, occupied by trees and grass and concrete and people. People like Blaire, who would offer water to a random stranger, who would take a moment to comfort that same stranger after he claimed to have lost a sibling. Blaire, whose genuine empathy couldn't be faked. Couldn't be scripted.

As he took it all in, as he stared into the calming eyes of his boothmate, Grey knew that the only fake element of this place was him, a guy hanging onto a lie to garner unearned sympathy. Ever the desperate chameleon parading as a peacock.

Don't forget to like and subscribe.

"Larry's sister Isabelle went missing about a year ago," Blaire said.

"I know. He told me last night."

"That's surprising. He doesn't talk about Isabelle that often."

"Isabelle ... that's a pretty name."

"She was a pretty girl—*is* a pretty girl." Blaire shook her head. "I noticed this look on his face when you told us your sister had gone missing too. It was like something clicked. Like he felt this connection to you."

"Am I interrupting something?" Johnson said, snatching Grey's attention.

Blaire slid her hand away from Grey's quickly. "You try to flush that doll down the toilet? Don't tell me you're scared now." She gave him a mocking frown.

In the second it took Johnson to reply—a microscopic, nearly imperceptible moment—Grey realized that Johnson had been clocking Blaire's hand. He'd seen Blaire's hand on top of Grey's. And the droopy expression on Johnson's face told Grey he wasn't too happy about it.

Johnson recovered. "Are you kidding? You know how much that thing'll be worth if this movie makes it big?" He patted

Grey's shoulder. "Hey, bro. Sorry I brought up your dead sister back there—"

"Missing," Blaire corrected.

"Uh, right. Missing. But it got us in the door and led to some sweet frickin' footage, right?"

"You're welcome?" Grey said.

Johnson's gaze shot past Grey and through the window. "Oh, shit. What's goin' on out there?"

Grey swiveled his head to see a Ram truck with four white guys hanging out of each window, mouths agape, shouting at Larry and Caleb.

Larry stepped out of the van, and as he did, so too did the truck's driver. His thick paint-colored boots pounded the cracked concrete of the parking lot, holding up the man's bulky frame. He was thick in that good-ole-boy kind of way—raised on meat and potatoes and a hard day's work.

But as the driver approached, Grey realized he wasn't squaring up to Larry.

He was trying to get *past* Larry.

And he was pointing toward Caleb.

Blaire said what they all must have been thinking. "He wants to take our footage."

Grey had *really* been looking forward to that slice of cranberry pie.

THE LOCALS

GREY COULDN'T GET TO the door fast enough, but Johnson had a runner's sprint and was out of the diner before Grey could shimmy his way out of the booth. The last thing they needed was to start some small-town turmoil, and a skirmish with anything other than the Witch could turn this entire film inside out.

Grey *had* to finish the film. And this fool was screwing with it.

"Is Johnson a fighter?" Grey asked Blaire as he ran to the door.

She answered, "He's a bit of a hothead, but I've never seen him get into a—"

Grey shot through the diner entrance before she had a chance to finish.

In the parking lot, Johnson had already shoved the driver off of Larry, and while Larry fiddled with his glasses, the three other good ole boys hopped out of the truck, slamming their doors shut in a weird display of ... machismo? From their body shapes to their straight-fit clothing, they each had a build like a soda can. One sported a hefty bowl that gave the top half of his body a mushroom shape. Another was decked out in freckles and was missing a tooth. But the man those two stood behind was bigger and broader than any of them. A clear alpha, if such a thing existed in fake rural America.

"'Ey! Fuck off!" Johnson shouted.

"Not until you gimme whatever's on that damn camera!" the driver shouted back, aiming his finger at a sheepish Caleb.

"The footage is ours, dumbass," Johnson said. "You can't just go around stealin' other people's shit."

The driver grinned, hawked up a loogie, and spit. "I've seen people like you out here before. Tryin' to exploit honest people."

"We're not exploiting anyone," Blaire chimed in.

"The men are talkin' now, sweetheart," the driver said.

Blaire grunted. "Excuse me?"

"We haven't done anything wrong," Larry said. "We got every participant to sign a release form."

"The hell is a release form?" the driver asked. "You big city types love to throw around bullship terms to make yourselves seem educated or somethin'. Whatever that sand monkey over there is holdin', I'm gonna take it and smash it."

"Sand monkey?" Caleb said. "Dude, I'm Puerto Rican."

Johnson took three quick steps toward the shouting man. "What did you just say to my boy?"

Grey darted after Johnson, making himself a barrier.

"Your boy? What are you two, gay wads or somethin'? Get outta my face." The man curled his fists.

Johnson only got closer.

As the man's elbow bent, winding up for a swift punch into Johnson's dumb broad jaw, Grey nudged Johnson out of the way in time for the driver's knuckles to miss their intended target.

Instead, they landed on Grey's left cheekbone.

A chorus of shouts from either side erupted. Grey prepared for the two parties to converge as he held his newly dented cheek.

CHKK-CHKK.

The crowd went silent.

Grey turned to see Martha Mae in a still frame straight out of an exploitation movie. She held her chin up defiantly, holding a shotgun diagonally across her body. The entrance door swung shut behind her as an empy shotgun shell toppled—*CLINK, CLINK, CLINK*—down the steps.

Where the hell are we? Grey thought.

"Elvis!" Martha Mae yelled. "You stop harassin' our visitors, goddammit! Ain't you got some houses need fixin' up?"

"Sorry, Martha Mae," Elvis (*Really?*) responded.

"Sorry?" Larry said. "Where I come from, what you just did is called assault."

"Let me guess: Your daddy's a lawyer?" Elvis responded.

"Would you shut your trap, Elvis?!" Martha shouted. "Don't think I won't call your daddy up!"

"We're pressing charges," Larry said.

"No," Grey interjected, the side of his face so numb he wondered if a bruise had already started to form. "That's not necessary." Wincing, he locked eyes with Elvis. "Just a misunderstanding, right? No big deal."

Elvis took a moment, looking like a bull behind the gate at a rodeo, then nodded. "Just a misunderstanding." When he said it, he changed the pitch of his voice, mocking Grey.

"Alright then," Larry said.

Switching back to his normal, manly-man voice, Elvis added, "But I'm givin' y'all a fair warnin' ... Don't go diggin' up this Witch of Hope Hollow mess if you know what's good fer ya. You might not like what you find. There's people who don't want you here. You think we just showed up?" He smirked. "Naw, we got a tip from a concerned citizen."

"That's enough," Martha Mae said. "I got customers to feed. Go on now."

The crew took their time to file back into the truck like coins being sucked into an old vacuum cleaner.

Grey waved to Martha Mae. "Thank you, miss."

She gave a wink and walked back inside.

Shotgun Waitress, Grey thought, his mind still stuck on that "exploitation film" track. *Trailer voice: They came to the wroooong diner.*

Grey had a feeling they'd been running into Elvis and his gang again, and if that happened in a different spot, they wouldn't have a Martha Mae to protect them.

When Elvis's van was out of sight, Larry whispered to Caleb, "Tell me you got that."

Caleb gave a sly grin and removed his coat from the top of a camera on the van floor, displaying a glowing red record button.

He'd been recording the entire exchange.

Larry smirked. "Hell yeah."

Blaire came to Grey's rescue, putting an arm around his shoulders. "Are you okay?"

"Yeah, totally fine. He doesn't hit that hard," Grey lied as he watched Elvis's truck sputtered down the road.

A figure appeared at the corner of the grime-covered convenience store across the street. Black sneakers, black pants, black shirt, long dark hair down to the shoulders.

No way ...

It couldn't have been ...

Was it?

Grey squinted his eyes, zoning on the figure's grim, toothless smile.

It was undeniably Rodney.

But before Grey could shout to him, Rodney stepped backward, disappearing behind the convenience store. It was performative and, oh, so obvious.

We got a tip from a concerned citizen, Elvis had said.

Grey now understood what he'd felt in his core when he saw the silver vest abandoned on the ground, when he saw the words written in the dirt and next to the sliding glass door. Rodney was playing the same game he was, pulling strings and manipulating the world of the film.

But he and Rodney weren't on the same team.

THE NIGHTMARE

It was dark by the time the crew had arrived back at the cabin. Caleb got to work unloading an entire day's worth of footage on a seemingly limitless SD card. Grey wasn't exactly a videography expert, but he knew a single card wouldn't have lasted the entire day, especially not with the run-and-gun style they'd used to shoot.

Holding a plastic bag filled with ice cubes against his face, Grey approached Caleb at the dinner table, which he'd outfitted as a technology command center of sorts—hard drives, film equipment, monitors, and a snaking assembly of cords.

"Hey, Caleb," Grey said, "did you, uh ... Did you happen to change out the battery at all while we were out today?"

Caleb stared at the ceiling, *reeeeaaaallly* thinking on it. "Nope, can't say that I did."

They'd been shooting for *seven hours*.

"No battery change all day?" Grey asked. "Seems pretty unlikely, right?"

Caleb shrugged. "Yep, pretty amazing, I guess."

"That was smart work with Elvis and the crew. How were you able to turn the camera on and get the lens aimed just right without them knowing?"

Caleb giggled. "I do a lot of guerrilla filmmaking, man. You learn how to be sneaky. The best footage happens when the camera's off, so I just try to film everything. It's the difference between getting paid to do documentaries and just shooting wedding videos to scrape by."

"Is that what you wanna do? Go around the world shooting stuff like this?" Grey asked.

"I want to make my own documentaries, yeah. I'm running camera, sure, but this is basically a mentorship opportunity. I like all this spooky stuff, hokey as it might be, so I'm hoping this can lead to some kind of series pitch, you know? *Urban Legends of the Midwest*, or something."

"That's really cool, Caleb," Grey said. "I really hope that works out for you."

"Crazier things have happened." Caleb shrugged.

"'Ey, broski," Johnson called to Grey from the living room. "Can I get a word with you?"

"Sure, what's up?" Grey walked over to the couch to sit opposite Johnson, preparing for another round of macho tomfoolery. He removed the bag from his cheek.

"Damn. Looks like you got a good shiner there," Johnson said.

"You should see the other guy," Grey replied.

"I did see the other guy."

"No, it's a ... Wait, are you serious?" Grey could see from Johnson's statue-still face that, yes, he was very serious. "Never mind."

"Look, man ... It was really dumb doing what you did. You know, steppin' in front of that punch. I mean, I could have taken it. Wouldn't've been my first fight."

"Thanks. I don't feel incredibly smart about it."

"Why'd you shove me out of the way? I've been an asshole to you. You don't even know me. Figured you would have loved to see that guy smash my face in."

He thought Grey was trying to protect him. Grey hadn't even put that much thought into it. He wasn't even thinking when he saw Elvis wind up for the punch. It was a quick, knee-jerk reaction that he just went for.

"Honestly, man, I don't know. I guess I just saw a guy about to get punched and didn't want it to happen. Not to you or anyone else."

Johnson nodded. "You're okay, Grady."

"It's Grey."

"Whatever. I don't say thanks very often."

Grey grinned. "You don't have to. Does my face look cool, at least?"

Johnson gave a tiny chuckle, and it was the most relaxed Grey had seen him in the small amount of time he'd known Johnson. "Yeah. It looks pretty cool."

Blaire joined them with a glass jar of purple liquid. Kombucha, if Grey had to guess. "You boys plannin' a cage match with the local hillbillies?"

"Johnson was giving me some tips for my next street fight," Grey responded. "So, are we gonna sit around telling ghost stories tonight?"

She took a swig. "I'm pretty wiped out. Probably heading off to bed soon."

"I'll prep the truck," Grey said without a single hint of irony. "You know, it's really not that bad in there. I've had worse sleeping arrangements."

"Oh, please, don't sleep in the truck again," Blaire said. "We have plenty of room in here." She made her voice louder. "That okay with everyone?"

Larry came out of the hallway in flannel bottoms and a t-shirt, drying off his hair with a towel. "Fine by me. I'm more worried about Johnson. He's the one who's cursed."

"Shut up, man," Johnson said. "I wish a witch *would* come at me."

"Guys, it's really okay," Grey said. "I insist. I'm fine sleeping in the van tonight. I appreciate you all keeping me involved in this. I think you're going to make something really great."

He would just need to double- and triple-check that the van was locked in case Rodney had any more surprises in store for him.

That night, Grey dreamed longer than he ever had. A nonstop nightmare that he was helpless to control. In it, he was wandering through the woods, tumbling over branches, bare feet crunching leaves. Running in the direction of screams. Screams that he knew to be from Cassandra and little Michael. With no light to guide him, he pinballed from tree to tree, shouting, shouting, shouting.

"Where are you?!" he would yell, but they'd only keep screaming, the tones changing directions. Every time he turned and ran through another gaggle of trees, the screams would shift as if the pair were teleporting, unstuck from all geography.

Every so often, he'd come across a tall woman in a black gown and a black veil and stop. The moonlight would only emerge when she was present, to display the outline of her frame, her glowing white eyes that pierced through her veil.

"Save them," she said in a voice that carried through the forest and echoed off the trees. A voice that might as well have been inside Grey's head. "Find the house of stone ... The house that appears to those who seek it."

THE MISSING CREW MEMEBER

THE VAN DOOR SLID open, springing Grey awake.

"Johnson's gone," Blaire said.

"W–wha–" Grey mumbled in a sleepy stupor.

"It's five o'clock," Blaire informed him. "We all overslept. Come inside."

"What? How?" Grey blinked the day into existence just quickly enough to see Blaire's black hair drift away. He winced, realizing he'd rolled over onto his swollen cheek in his sleep, and picked himself up off the van floor quickly.

"Come on!" Blaire yelled from the porch.

Grey stumbled as he followed her inside. Larry wobbled around in the living room, rubbing his eyes in a dumbfounded state.

"Grey, did you hear anything last night?" Larry asked.

Grey looked around, clocking Blaire and Caleb. "Uh, no. It's–it's five p.m.?" Grey asked.

"Yeah. We all just woke up," Caleb said.

"But ... how's that possible? I haven't slept that long since, like ..." Grey *really* thought on it. "... ever."

"It's not," Larry answered. "And we can't find Johnson. Left his phone and wallet. Suitcase is still in his room."

Blaire darted into the hallway …

And re-entered the living room, waving the hair-doll in the air. "And he left this behind."

"Don't touch that!" Caleb commanded. "Put it down!"

"So you're really starting to believe in all this?" Blaire asked. "This is *Johnson* we're talking about. He's probably messing with us, right?"

"One of my cameras is gone too," Caleb said. "No reason for him to take that. He has no idea how to work it."

As the crew deliberated, Grey inspected the interior of the house. Nothing seemed too out of the ordinary. The chairs were under the table. The furniture was exactly how it had been left the night before. But the sliding glass door at the end of the living room, spread open, caught his eye.

"Guys …" Grey said. They all stopped talking and turned to him. "Did anybody open the screen door?"

No one answered.

Grey approached the opening cautiously, getting a full, unobstructed view of the tree line at the back of the house.

He stepped out onto the grass, then turned to inspect the sliding glass door. But he didn't have to study it for very long. On the side of the house written in mud was a message that was becoming familiar.

THE WITCH LIVES

Larry joined Grey outside.

"Shit ... You think it was those idiots at the diner?" Larry asked.

It could've been. But Grey's gut told him differently. He knew Rodney was out there, armed with the knowledge of this world. He'd seen Rodney, and Rodney had seen *him*. And he knew Rodney despised him. "I have no idea."

"We should go see the sheriff and report it," Larry said.

"I'll bring the camera," Caleb said, standing. He paused before adding, "Actually ... I have an idea."

THE SHERIFF

Sheriff Daniel Bobbit was a bald man with a wide gut, which he used as a shelf of sorts for his hands as he leaned back in his chair. The desk Bobbit sat behind was solid wood, heavy and chipped, and looked like it had been sinking into the coffee-stained carpet since before Grey was alive. "Now, I was just about to head home for the night, but my receptionist told me a group came in sayin' a visitor went missin'. I knew it was y'all. The documentary crew tryin' to make a movie about our little witch. Think you're the first?"

Grey stood at one end of the horseshoe comprised of the crew. He tried desperately not to eye the button camera Caleb had hidden in his shirt. It did actually look more like a camera lens than a button, but Sheriff Bobbit, rounding the corner on sixty soon and sitting behind a generations-old desktop computer, seemed like the type to call into tech support because he didn't know his PC was unplugged.

He wouldn't know the difference.

"And call it double-luck," the man said with a Southern twang. "I had plans to go on patrol about an hour ago, until I saw we had an anonymous donation. A half dozen body cams.

Can you believe that? Some generous citizen donated body cameras to this tiny operation." He smiled, genuinely touched.

Grey *couldn't* believe it, and he also couldn't shake the feeling that this "generous donation" had some correlation to his arrival. Body cameras meant more mixed media, more angles, more footage.

"We don't get anything in terms of budget in Hope Hollow," Sheriff Bobbit continued. "Some good people in these parts, let me tell ya."

Larry said, "Sir—"

"Sheriff, if you will," Sheriff Bobbit interrupted.

"Sheriff, sorry." Larry cleared his throat, visibly nervous. "Our friend is gone, and someone left a warning on the side of our rental. There was a bit of an altercation outside the diner yesterday."

Sheriff Bobbit grinned at Grey, and it felt as if the man was poking at the bulb on Grey's cheek with his eyes. "Is that so?"

"Okay, so you're aware?" Grey asked.

"I'm aware there weren't any charges pressed."

Blaire grunted. "This is pointless, guys. He's not gonna help us."

"You'd be wise to respect me, young woman," Bobbit said.

She approached his desk and pressed her palms against the wood grain, leaning over. "Do you always tap dance like this when people bring you crimes? Honestly, your feet must be sore at this point."

"You sure got a mouth on you, girl."

Larry took a step forward. Whether it was to be menacing or assertive, Bobbit didn't bite. "Are you gonna help us or not ... *Sheriff*?"

Bobbit sat up straight. Sighed. "You got signs of break-in?"

"Uh ... No," Larry admitted. "We definitely locked the doors at night, though. Especially after what happened at the diner."

Bobbit gave a shrug. "When'd y'all realize he was gone?"

"This morning," Larry said. "Well ... this afternoon. We all woke up late."

"Up all night partyin', huh?" Bobbit said.

"No," Blaire shot back, removing herself from the desk. "We might've been drugged. We have no idea. We all woke up around thirty minutes ago."

Sheriff Bobbit's expression changed. He grew serious as if Blaire had triggered something in him other than misogyny. "Wait now ... Y'all were all dead asleep and woke up in the middle of the day at the same time?"

"That's what I said," Blaire answered.

Bobbit leaned back in his chair again, this time further, causing it to squeak in resistance. "Y'all wouldn't try and scare an old man, would you?"

"What?" Blaire asked. "No, we're just telling you the facts."

"You see now, there are stories people 'round here tell about the Witch. Say she messes with your perception of time in an attempt to make ya go crazy. How does she do that? Well, she casts a spell on ya to make ya sleep. Seems like y'all got caught in that spell. Unless you're just foolin' around with me and tryin' to get some shit for your movie. If I find out you're recordin' this, I'll have all o' ya's prosecuted. Now, my hands are tied until your friend is gone for forty-eight hours. When that time comes, you come back here and we'll file a missin' persons report. I'll file it for ya, honest to God. But until that time ... y'all watch out for yourselves. 'Cause if ya ain't messin' with me ... if you've really been marked by the Hope Hollow Witch ... well, then you might've just brought chaos back to this town."

"You believe in all of this, don't you?" Larry asked.

The sheriff shrugged. "Don't matter what I do and don't believe, does it? Won't do much good to y'all when the Witch comes for ya. *If* she's real, that is. Now, it'll get dark soon. Y'all best be gettin' home."

Larry nodded. "Thank you for your time, Sheriff." He turned to leave, prompting the others to do the same.

"Y'all look like you could use a drink. Y'all drinkin' age, aren't ya? Head on over to the Thirsty Turtle 'bout five miles down the road. Tell whoever's at the bar that Sheriff Bobbit ordered your first round." He showed his teeth—yellow streaks dangling from whatever flesh was left of his gums. "Contrary to what you might think, we're hospitable to our outta-towners."

THE THIRSTY TURTLE

IT WASN'T A BAD idea, Grey reckoned. In a town like this with nothing to do, there'd be a slew of folks at the Thirsty Turtle, they could all shove phone screens in front of.

They all agreed not to take Bobbit's offer to buy their first round. Caleb wasn't twenty-one yet, for starters, and Grey didn't have his ID on him. Still, they all seemed to agree that it was a trap. They didn't know *how* it was a trap. Didn't know what kind of backwoods Rube Goldberg machine of shittiness they'd set off by telling the bartender that the Sheriff sent them. Larry and Blaire got their own drinks instead, if only to keep attention off their missing person investigation.

Cheers ...

"Have you seen this person?"

A couple sips ...

"Hey, have you seen this guy? Six-five, broad shoulders?"

Time to use the John ...

"We're looking for our friend. Did you happen to see him?"

All the while, Grey snacked on a bucket of fries—the once frozen, then deep-fried kind—with Caleb, his sober buddy for the day.

Caleb shook his head. "What an asshole."

"The sheriff?" Grey asked.

"No, Johnson," Caleb answered. "I have a feeling this is all just one big prank, and look at everything we're doing for him now. It's almost like ... I'd be pissed if he *wasn't* missing ... That sheriff *was* an asshole, though."

"Bit of a stereotype, right?" Grey replied.

"What do you mean?"

"Redneck sheriff, overweight, misogynist, spends his days sitting at a desk in a middle of nowhere town. Reminds me of every backwoods horror movie ever made."

"Made for good footage, at least," Caleb said, pointing to his button camera.

"What other cool gadgets do you have back at the cabin?"

"Well ... after what happened last night ..." Caleb leaned in, wiping fryer grease on his jacket. "I'm only tellin' you this because you're sleeping in the van and can't mess with any of the equipment when we're locked inside. I got five security cameras I'm gonna set up around the house when everyone's sleeping. Stashed them under my bed when everyone was unpacking, just in case. I brought a hotspot I can pair 'em with, too. Wireless means you need Bluetooth recording to the cloud. In a place like this, the Internet could go down whenever."

Grey grinned. "Dang. You prepared for everything. But why the secrecy?"

"Surveillance works best if the surveilled don't know about it. Blaire's my girl; she wouldn't do anything to fabricate this documentary. Johnson, like I said, can be a bit of a prankster. Still can't rule him out. But Larry ... I feel like that dude's got some darkness to him."

"How do you mean?"

"I know some kids who took courses with him before his sister went missing—"

"Isabelle."

"Oh, you know? He doesn't talk about it much."

"So I've heard."

"Anyway, they said before he was this fun-loving dude. Everyone's favorite film professor. But now, the guy's just neutral. Direct. Sometimes he just feels kinda off. I know the guy lost his sister, but ... maybe that's a reason to think he might be compelled to do something a bit, I don't know ..."

"Nefarious?"

Caleb nodded. "That's a good word for it. Anyways, we never had this conver—"

Conflicting scents of dried paint and cheap cologne wafted from over Grey's shoulder. As soon as the strange mix registered in Grey's nose, Caleb's expression shifted. He didn't like who or what he was seeing behind Grey.

And when that who-or-what said, "Fancy seein' you boys here," Grey knew they had a problem. That smell, that good ole boy accent, the assembly of boot-scuffing footsteps behind him ... It could only be one guy.

"Heard y'all paid my daddy a visit today," Elvis said.

This was the trap.

Grey, Larry, Caleb, and Blaire—they were mice, scurrying around this maze of a bar.

They'd gone after the cheese ...

Contrary to what you might think, we're hospitable to our outta-towners, Bobbit had said. Grey hadn't considered that he might have a deranged idea of hospitality.

SNAP! The metal had flipped over, coming down on their helpless rodent necks like a sledgehammer on a tube of toothpaste.

"Who's your dad?" Caleb said, his mouth hanging open. He wasn't scared, just a little dumb.

"The Sheriff, I'm assuming," Grey said as he scooched slowly out of the booth, wiping French fry oil on his shirt.

Grey turned to face Elvis and his home maintenance henchmen, Freckles and Bowl Cut, their clothes slathered in paint and grime in a way fitting of an L.A. catwalk.

Elvis winced, "Ooooo. You're the one I popped in the cheek."

"Does it look kinda cool, though?" Grey asked.

Ignoring the question, Elvis said, "Heard y'all was lookin' for your friend."

"We are," Caleb said from behind Grey. "You wouldn't happen to know where he is, would you?"

Elvis turned back to Freckles and Bowl Cut and chuckled. As if given permission to do so, they chuckled too. "Why the hell would I know where he is? Far as I'm concerned, one down, just ..." He thought long and hard, then landed on, "... a few more to go."

"Why are you being so hostile?" Grey asked. "We haven't done anything to you."

"But you will," Elvis replied. "We get folks like you all the time. Podcasters, paranormal investigators, YouTubers, they're all the same. Just want a taste of that fame teet. Want to exploit good, honest people who live in Hope Hollow. Got to a point where I had to stop letting that happen. Can you guess how many of them go missin'?"

Elvis lifted up his shirt, revealing the silver handle of a pistol hanging out the top of his trousers. No holster, just tucked behind the fabric as if it were taking a nap, all the while aimed at Elvis' manhood.

Satisfied that Grey and Caleb had gotten a good look at what he was packing, Elvis lowered his shirt.

Where was Martha Mae when they needed her?

Can't finish the movie if I'm dead.

"We were just leaving," Grey said.

"Great, we'll walk you out," Elvis replied.

Just then, heavy footsteps slapped the hardwood flooring behind Grey.

"What's goin' on here?" It was Larry.

Followed by Blaire. "You guys again. You been stalking us? Did you do something to our friend?"

"You must be talkin' 'bout the big guy," Elvis said. "Seemed like he could handle himself. That is, until training wheels here stepped in to take a punch for 'im?"

Elvis aimed a grin Grey's way.

Training wheels? Grey was too confused to respond.

"We don't know what happened to your friend," Elvis said. "Maybe he took my advice and left town. You lot shoulda done the same."

Grey turned back toward Larry. "We need to go *now.*" Then, he mouthed the word *gun* and bent his arm at a ninety-degree angle, pretending to fire two shots with his thumb.

"We'll come with ya," Elvis said. "The night's young. Let's have ..." He eyed Blaire and bit his lip. "... a little fun."

"What—" Blaire said before Grey cut her off.

"No thanks, we're good." Grey put his arms around the three of them—Larry and Blaire in one arm, Caleb in the other—in an attempt to usher them out.

Grey lowered his voice. "He's the sheriff's son. I'm pretty sure he wants to kill us. Get in the car and drive."

"No shit?" Blaire responded.

"It's true," Caleb whispered. "He basically said he disappears out-of-towners."

Elvis and Hillbillies One and Two matched their pace behind Grey.

Still walking toward the exit, Grey said, "Seriously, guys, we're good. We're getting out of your hair and leaving town. You won't see us again."

"Too late for that," Elvis said.

"What do we do?" Caleb asked.

Larry stopped their progress. "I'll talk to them. Probably just a misunderstanding."

"Dude, you don't understand," Caleb pleaded.

Elvis halted behind them, a shit-eating-and-loving-it grin plastered on his face.

"No ... we have to play along," Grey said.

"What do you mean?" Larry asked.

"Shh. I got this." Grey turned back to Elvis and the boys, praying that this gambit paid off while simultaneously weighing the likelihood of these goons decorating him with red badges of courage and dumping him in a deep, deep hole. If they were serious—and they sure *looked* serious—was this entire cursed game rigged against him?

Screw that. So long as there was breath in his lungs and a town mythology perpetuated by superstition, Grey could rig the game in his favor.

"Guess your dad didn't tell you that we're marked, huh?" Grey said.

The droop of Elvis' face wasn't subtle enough to slip past Grey, nor was the sudden atrophy of the young man's limbs. *Marked.* The word had frozen Elvis in place.

"Whatchu mean?" Elvis asked.

"A doll made of hair showed up on the windowsill of the room Johnson was sleeping in two nights ago. We all thought it was the townspeople messin' with us. Could've been you three for all we know." Grey shrugged.

Elvis tried to play it cool, but the two guys behind him weren't so slick. Their jaws unlocked, each chin slowly making its way to the scuffed-up flooring.

Grey continued. "I woke up late today—like, *really* late. Too late. Come to find out, we all woke up late around the same time. Almost like we were all under some kind of spell. That's when we noticed that our friend was missing."

"You're lyin'," Elvis said.

"Am I?" Grey replied. "You better be sure I am. Because I'm guessing by the looks on your partners' faces that you all don't like the prospect of spending the night with four people with *that* kind of target on their backs."

Elvis swallowed, then cleared his throat. He may have had the gun, but Grey had the power.

"Y'all go on and leave town, then," Elvis said. "Best not be seein' you again. If I do—"

"You won't," Grey interrupted, slowly backing away.

Satisfied that Elvis wasn't following them, the crew shuffled quickly out of the bar and toward the van, kicking up gravel on their way.

"That was brave what you did," Blaire told Grey before stepping into the van.

Larry patted Grey's shoulder. "Using their superstition against them. Smart. You might just be our guardian angel, Grey."

"Nah. I've just seen a lot of small-town horror movies," Grey replied. The problem was, however, that none of those movies gave him any kind of blueprint for where to go from here.

THE STICKY NOTE

Grey's head was full of wheels—spinning, spinning, spinning—as he tried to figure out how to progress the version of *The Witch of Hope Hollow* that he'd been dropped into. All of the pieces were there, but the whole, as of yet, wasn't entirely satisfying. There *must* be something else left to discover.

Something big.

Something disturbing.

Something having to do with Johnson.

Something having to do with Rodney.

Grey considered whether he would need to venture out into the woods with nothing but his wits and a fire poker—toss up a Hail Mary in hopes that he could find either of those elusive figures.

A sign of hope—or maybe doom—revealed itself when Grey followed the crew into the living room of their rental and Caleb muttered, "Uh ... That wasn't there when we left, right?"

A video camera was sitting on the coffee table—the same coffee table they'd gathered around before seeing Sheriff Bobbit. When they'd left, there was nothing on its surface, and now, this camera was smack dab in the middle of it. The only thing missing was a yellow sticky note with the words "PLAY ME".

Caleb went to inspect it.

"Is it the one you lost last night?" Larry asked.

Caleb turned it in his hands. "Yeah." He sat and flipped open the viewfinder, then sifted through the footage. "There's a video on here that was taken last night."

"*When* last night?" Blaire asked.

"When we were all asleep?" Grey asked.

Instead of answering, nodding, or otherwise acknowledging Grey's question, Caleb's eyes tilted back down toward the camera.

"Let's run a cable to your laptop," Larry ordered. "I have a feeling we'll all need to see this."

The Witch of Hope Hollow
Timecode: 49:32:11

Everyone huddles around Caleb's laptop. One of the USB ports runs a cord to the camera that was previously sitting in the middle of the table.

Caleb presses play.

On the laptop screen, Johnson's face appears in a circle of light, but not the strong, macho-presenting fool. It's a bug-eyed, wild version of Johnson, panting, shaking, scared out of his mind.

"Is it recording?" Johnson asks. "Is it … Yeah, it's recording. Okay. Look, guys, I can't wake any of you up. I've been trying, but your asses are dead-ass asleep. Look."

Johnson spins the camera around and opens a bedroom door. The camera beams into the dark room. He approaches a bed where a body rests under the covers. He comes closer to reveal the serene face of Larry, eyes closed and on his side, fast asleep.

"Larry!" Johnson says. He nudges Larry. Shoves him. Slaps his cheek. Then, he turns the camera back toward his face.

"It's like this with all of you. You won't wake up, and I keep hearing something outside. I thought it might've been Grady or whatever out in the van, but it's coming from the other side of the house. It's coming from the woods—Wait …" He tilts his chin up. "There it is again." He speedwalks through the hallway. "I'm comin' for you, you son of a bitch!"

Johnson turns the camera around so it's facing ahead of him. It wobbles as he sprints out of the hallway and through the living room. "You think you can mess with us?! Huh?!"

Johnson slows as he gets to the living room. His voice lowers. "What … w-what are you saying?" He listens. "God, I don't know if the camera's picking this up, but the fucker's whispering something about the woods. He wants me to go out there."

The camera light reflects a yellow orb on the sliding glass door. A mirror version of Johnson enlarges as he comes closer to the glass. The trees beyond the glass pane create a disorienting half-Johnson, half-woods image.

A childlike giggle reverberated from behind the camera.

Johnson whips the camera around, capturing nothing but the dark living room in the light. "Fuck … Is someone in here? Guys! Would someone WAKE THE HELL UP?!"

The sliding glass door slices open behind him.

"Shit!" He turned the camera back around to the sliding glass door. Wind whistles in through the opening.

"Who did that?!"

Johnson's breath quickens—*PANT, PANT, PANT.*

"Alright, wanna mess with me, bitch? Yeah, let's go."

He steps out into the backyard.

Checks left.

Checks right.

Turns the camera back on the tree line fifteen feet ahead of him and walks forward.

"Who's out there?!" he shouts. "Stop bein' a bitch and come face me!"

The yellow glow of the camera light dances on the trees, catching bark and leaves in its radius…

Until it lands on something different. An object that isn't a tree or a twig. Maybe something that's not even animal. Not even human.

A pale leg, impossibly long and bent at ninety degrees in the wrong direction, bearing weight on an old, beat-up leather shoe. As soon as the light hit it, the thing scurries away in a rustle of leaves.

That same childish giggle chimes again.

"What the fuck was that?" Johnson's full-blown panicking now. Lost all control of his breathing.

He scans the woods with the camera light. Whatever was walking on a bent leg is gone.

"Screw this. I'm going inside." Johnson turns …

But stops when the camera catches something in the distance, away from the treeline. Under moonlight and a thick tuft of fog, a dark figure stands like a shadow turned solid.

Johnson screams. "What do you want?"

He waits silently.

Then, "What?"

And, finally, "Okay … okay … I'll go to the house."

The screen goes black.

THE FIGURE

Caleb turned in his chair to face the group hovering around him and asked Larry, "You don't remember getting slapped in the face?"

"I'm not a heavy sleeper, Caleb. Any little movement wakes me up."

"Some crazy shit is happening here," Blaire said.

"Like, for example ..." Grey motioned forward. "Mind if I take over here?"

"Knock yourself out," Caleb said, rolling backward in his chair to make way for Grey. "Just don't delete anything."

Grey ran his fingertip over the mousepad. Clicked and dragged, taking the playhead backward and causing a discombobulation succession of video frames. He found the spot he was looking for and stopped.

"What the hell is that?" Blaire asked.

Through the trees, a long—*impossibly* long—leg was bent the opposite way. Now that he had a better look at it, Grey could see a boot below the ankle and a dirty pair of pants ripped off at the knee—that same knee that was buckled in a way that made him question where the damn knee cap even was inside the skin.

"Do you think it's ..." Blaire didn't finish. *Couldn't* finish.

"Willie Long Legs," Larry said.

A mix between a grunt and a laugh forced its way out of Caleb's throat. "Get the fuck out, man."

"The locals warned us about the acolytes, right?" Larry said. "That right there ... That might be the first video proof of Willie Long Legs. The spider boy."

A chill went down Grey's spine. It wasn't just that the leg was deformed; it was long and thin, standing about six feet before the bend. A true abomination. If that was just one quarter of its body, Grey loathed to imagine what Willie would look like in his entirety.

He shook the chill away and pressed forward, knowing there were more clues to uncover. "And then who is this?" Grey moved the playhead again, this time stopping on a frame of the dark figure standing outside the woods. "Even if we upped the exposure, we wouldn't be able to make out any features. It's completely dark. Looks humanoid, though. They say the Witch tries to recruit new helpers, right? Maybe whoever this is—"

Rodney, Grey thought.

"—maybe this is someone new."

"And whoever it is," Larry said, "they have one of my students."

"I'll go to the house ..." Blaire added, mimicking Johnson's final moments in the footage.

The group went silent.

"I had a dream last night," Blaire continued. "Freaked me out. I was running through the woods—"

"Holy shit," Caleb interjected. "Did you hear ... screaming? Like, no matter where you went, no matter how far you ran—"

"The screams never got closer or farther away," Grey said.

Bewildered, Blaire muttered, "What? Did we all have the same dream?"

"I heard my sister," Larry said. "She was crying. I kept running, trying to find her, and I just couldn't get to her."

"Did you all see a woman dressed in black, too?" Grey asked.

"The house appears to those who seek it," Blaire said.

Caleb gasped. "That's what she told me in the dream. It was freaky as shit."

"It was the Witch," Larry said.

Grey peered past the sliding glass door. The woods loomed beyond the clear pane, endless and foreboding, with branches like crooked arms ready to snatch each of them up, welcoming them to the infinite darkness.

As Grey studied the deep, dark woods, Larry's voice droned on, somehow becoming lower, drowned out by the sounds of the woods. The bugs, the shuffle of leaves, the snapping of twigs. How could he hear it so clearly?

"As of this moment," Larry said, "everyone needs to operate on the assumption that all of this is real. All the dumb myths the townsfolk said, the weird little voodoo doll, the sleep spell, all of it."

"So you really think Johnson wandered into the woods, looking for some Schroedinger's Cat house that exists but also doesn't?" Caleb said.

"How can you still be so skeptical?" Blaire asked.

The group continued on as a low shriek pierced Grey's ear. Steadily, it became louder ...

Louder ...

A series of screams rising as if someone was twisting a dial. It was coming from two voices—Grey knew it. And the cries for help solidified it.

Cassandra and Michael.

Well-played, Witch.

Once he'd come to his senses, he realized the group had devolved into pandemonium—each of them trying to speak over one another like animals fighting for scraps.

"Hey!" Grey shouted, silencing the crew. "Larry's right. The Witch is out there, toying with us. The only way we beat this thing is by outsmarting it."

"What do you mean, 'beat this thing'?" Larry asked.

"I–I don't know yet," Grey said. "Not exactly. We know the Witch visited each of us in a dream and basically gave us an open invitation to come find her. So we seek out the house."

"Right. We find the house, we find Johnson," Blaire said.

Caleb sighed. "He's an asshole, but he's *our* asshole."

"As his professor, I'm responsible for Johnson's safety," Larry said.

Blaire sighed. "And based on that video, let's be honest ... We're no safer here than we are out there."

"Wait, Larry, are we going into the woods to find Johnson, or do you think ..." Caleb trailed off.

Grey had an idea of what he was planning to say—the words that got lodged in Caleb's throat. Grey locked eyes with Blaire, and he knew what she was thinking, too. Her belief in this new reality filled with curses and spells and monsters melded with the reality Grey had created for himself. She was thinking Grey's sister—the one he'd told her was lost to the Hope Hollow woods—might be in that same house that they were planning to search for. Just like Larry had come to a similar conclusion about his own sister. Grey nodded and said:

"Let's go."

"Whoa, guys, this is getting kinda nuts," Caleb protested. "We're talking about an *imaginary* house. How do we know that footage wasn't faked?"

Blaire threw her hands in the air as if wrapping her arms around some mammoth solidification of her frustration. "Who the hell in this town could fake that? We're stuck in the dust bowl here. And you *know* Johnson can't do shit with special effects. That leg was real, man."

"You can stay," Larry said to Caleb. "We'll take your camera equipment and go on our own. But imagine what you might miss if that imaginary house is real. Imagine the footage someone else'll have to take credit for ... *if* it's real."

Caleb drew a long breath, the gears of his consciousness grinding as he weighed the possibility of the impossible. "Let's gear up," he said. "We bring everything we can carry. Back up batteries, a second camera, food and drink, everything."

"Attaboy," Larry said.

Blaire's eyes landed on Grey. "You know you don't have to come. Finding Johnson is on us."

"Actually," Larry cut in. "Grey might be the most important part of this."

A pain shot through Grey's gut, similar to how seeing a police car in his rearview would make his body tense irrationally. What did Larry know?

"And why is that?" Grey asked.

"You saw the house that night we found you. Didn't you?"

Grey thought back to those tense few seconds after he'd picked himself up off the grass, recalling that vine-covered stone fortress shrouded in moonglow like some cartoonish Midwestern version of Dracula's castle.

He was actually embarrassed that Larry had come to the conclusion before him.

Grey nodded. Then, mustering any amount of bravado he could offer, Grey said, "Let's go."

In fact, every rational fiber of Grey's being said going into the woods at night was a BAD IDEA. But this was a horror movie. Horror movie characters weren't known for making rational decisions. And that's how Grey knew it was the perfect decision to make.

THE WOODS

THIS WAS THE PART where they'd fumble through the forest. Eventually, they'd get split up. Maybe they'd end up with two parties, each with their own camera. It might've been a perfect scenario considering Caleb's backup camera bag. Maybe one party would find the house first. Maybe Johnson would be inside of it. Maybe they'd scamper around, catching tiny snippets of the Witch's ghouls on camera. And then, just when things were getting *really* tense, the second party would show up. Maybe that would be Grey and Blaire. Why did he imagine himself with Blaire? Was he growing fond of her just because of her unconditional kindness, or was it something more—

Focus, Grey!

He could easily help see this film through, but that might come at the expense of their lives. Found footage movies rarely end with many survivors. Sometimes one or two, but oftentimes zero. The bar for a satisfying ending was so low, all he'd really need was a tense climax with a few good jump scares in dimly lit rooms.

He could high tail it out of there while everyone else got trapped.

Grey could be the lone survivor.

But Larry would never get his movie, and he certainly would never find his sister.

Caleb would never get to make *Urban Legends of the Midwest.*

Blaire would never prove to her family of white collar workers that what she was doing had merit.

And Johnson ... Screw Johnson. He was an asshole.

But why does he feel like *Grey's* asshole, too?

Caleb led the way, the beam of his camera light carving a path for the rest of the group, illuminating a monotonous rotation of trees and branches. The camera bag nestled on his back was like a turtle shell—stiff and bulky. Being the skeptic in the group, he was the most fit to lead. Unlike the rest of them, he had no anticipation of seeing some unnaturally lanky spider boy sifting through the leaves, knocking his bony knees against trees and branches in an attempt to scare them stupid.

After fifteen minutes of walking, though, Caleb was the first to question where they were even going. "So, do we just keep walking straight, or—"

"Shh, did you hear that?" Blaire said, tilting her head.

"Hear what?" Grey asked.

"I didn't hear anything," Caleb said.

Peering deep into the woods, eyes wide, Blaire said, "I'm grabbing the backup cam. Just in case, you know?" She darted toward the camera bag around Caleb's shoulders and unzipped it.

It's happening, Grey thought. *Let it happen. We're getting close to the climax.*

He'd be back with Cassandra and Michael soon.

Blaire turned the back-up camera on.

Flipped open the viewfinder.

And as soon as she turned the camera light on, Grey said, "You can't split up."

Blaire kept the camera low, putting a halo of light around her feet. "Yeah, we definitely shouldn't."

"We're not splitting up," Larry said.

"No, listen ..." *What are you doing?!* The voice inside Grey's head was throwing a fit. "... Blaire's probably going to hear that noise again. What did it sound like, Blaire?"

Blaire cocked her eyes side-to-side. "A scream, I think."

"The next time you hear it, it's gonna be more clear. You're gonna wanna sprint to it. We're all gonna follow you, maybe some of us make it to you, maybe some of us don't, maybe all of us do, I don't know, but if we panic, there's a good chance we don't make it out of these w—"

Thwack!

Grey leapt an inch off the ground, turning toward the sound of a meat cleaver cutting into flesh. "Okay, that one I definitely heard."

A shrill scream echoed through the woods, a deep, masculine voice pinballing from tree to tree. The voice of someone with a large presence...

Thwack!

... potentially being cut to pieces.

"Johnson!" Blaire sprinted past Grey, breaking from the group just as he'd predicted.

"Blaire, stop!" Grey yelled.

But it was too late to convince her otherwise. She ran deep into the woods, becoming a floating orb of light getting gradually smaller.

Caleb and Larry ran after her.

Grey had to keep them all together, despite his every instinct to let this all play out, to let them be the typical dumb, flat horror movie characters who fabricate their own demise.

He swung his right arm back, getting ready to throw it forward and propel him into a wimpy movement that fifth graders might've qualified as running—

Smack!

He fell sideways with a hard shoulder driving him toward the ground.

Grey rolled through the impact, shoving his attacker away and springing to his feet before the sting could set in his shoulder.

Standing there in the darkness, Grey could make out the outline of a short, scrawny man with matted hair running past his shoulders.

Rodney.

"You shouldn't be here," Rodney said.

"No shit, neither of us should," Grey fired back. "What the hell are you doing?"

"I'm doing the Witch's bidding, dumbass."

Another *THWAK* in the distance ...

Followed by a *SCREAM* ...

Maybe thirty yards away now, Blaire shouted, "Johnson!"

"Let me guess," Grey said. "That's acolyte number three, right? You're leading them to the Butcher."

Rodney seethed. "And *you* aren't going to ruin the plan."

"What is going on here? Look, I know we've had our, uh, differences or whatever, but this has to stop. You kidnapped one of the crew. Look at what you're doing now!"

"Don't pretend like you care about these people. They're not real."

"We *need* to start working together to get out of here."

"Get out? Why would I want to leave?"

"What?! You want to *stay* here?"

"Why the hell would I wanna go back? The real world's bullshit. There's a plan here. There's a beginning and a middle and an end. Rinse, repeat. The only difference is instead of putting up with shitty little weasels like you, I get to lead them to their deaths and watch them die over and over again."

Whoa, Grey thought. He'd sensed some darkness in Rodney before, but this was *DARK*-dark.

"I don't know what this place has done to you, but—"

"Stop getting in the way," Rodney said. "You haven't seen the film. I have. Lady Hyne wasn't supposed to get hurt in the first act. She scoops up Johnson and flies away."

"I knew it! He sucks way too much to stay in the movie long-term."

"You've thrown everything off. The crew is supposed to be down two people by now. Instead, we're working on taking out the second. If you continue interrupting the structure of the film, what do you think happens to you? The Witch doesn't want you. The best you can do is go back to the rental and let things play out. The movie isn't unsalvageable at this point. I'm trying to help you. I shouldn't, but I am."

"So I just do nothing and, what, allow them to be led to their deaths like you said?"

"They're not real, you imbecile! They mean nothing. They're projections of actual actors playing characters who didn't exist before all of this and won't exist after. Stop screwing with the plot! I don't know how you managed to maim Lady Hyne, but you might not be so lucky next time."

"What happens to them? What happens to the crew?"

"Why do you care?"

"You want me to stop interfering?" Grey said. "Tell me what happens, and I'll stop."

Rodney let out a deep, cold breath. "What do you think is gonna happen? They run around and lose each other. They run through the woods for hours and start to lose their grip on reality. They really start padding out the runtime. Then, eventually, everyone finds the mansion. The Witch uses all four of them as a sacrifice in the machine to bring her into the real world. Four souls in exchange for hers. The movie ends. You get to go home."

The machine, Grey thought. *Just like the locals said.*

"Then what happens to you?" Grey asked.

"We carry out this plan, then the Witch keeps me as an acolyte."

"What? Are you out of your mind?"

"Go back to the cabin, Grey! Go back to your shitty life and your shitty little Youtube channel. You were never supposed to see the Witch's lair."

I was never supposed to see ... what?

Grey's fingertips scanned the compass jutting out of his jeans pockets. He removed it and eyed the direction as it hovered over the big N.

Another scream came from that direction. The direction that the compass pointed in the first few moments, he'd found himself in a new world.

The one thing that connected him to the old world—to Michael—was leading him straight toward the Witch.

Grey imagined one day, sometime soon, telling Michael about this whole ordeal. Michael might be the only person who'd believe him. How would he tell Michael the story ended? With him packing it up for the night? Waiting for his story to end?

Nah.

One more look at that compass and he knew where he needed to go. He stuffed it back in his pocket.

"Screw your ending. We can make a better one. What you're planning here ... You don't wanna do it. Trust me. I've seen what happens when people stick around. I've seen what they become. You don't want that for yourself. And I think, deep down, you don't wanna kill these people, whether they're real or not."

"Oh, no, see, that's where you're wrong, Grey. I really do. No, I *like* it here. Back home, I was nothing. Less than nothing. I failed at everything. My Dad's been sick for so long because ... I don't know, whatever I tried, I just couldn't get the dosage. I even failed at killing him."

The admission hit Grey like a sledgehammer in the gut. "Rodney ..." The name slipped out. "... what are you—"

"My name's Ryan, asshole!"

No shit? So close...

Rodney (never Ryan, especially not now) pounced on Grey faster than he could react. Grey was still dumbstruck by the implication that Rodney had tried to kill his own father. It couldn't have been true, but, then again, he seemed pretty intent on killing Grey.

Before Grey registered what was happening, Rodney's wiry arm wrapped around his throat. Grey's head bent back, his windpipe shrinking in an inescapable chokehold. He fell backward onto Rodney as the man squeezed harder. How'd Grey let this puny bastard get the jump on him?

Rodney gave a sinister laugh, then hissed in his ear, "I know you read your comments. Guess what? I'm RollingShutter459. Your YouTube channel sucks, you talentless hack. Whatever adoration you get from those losers in the comment section is worth nothing. You won't be remembered for shit besides being a failure like me. At least I can change things here. This is *my* twist ending."

As his vision became an inky pool of darkness, the words "twist ending" repeated in his head.

THE SABATOGE

BOOM! BOOM! BOOM!

An onslaught of *thuds* rattled in Grey's skull like a bird in a shoebox as he opened his eyes and blinked, blinked, blinked, trying to awaken the world around him.

"Open up!" The voice sounded familiar. Gruff, older, with a hint of a southern twang.

With that southern twang came the image of yellow teeth and burly hands resting on a round belly.

Once his vision became clear, Grey realized he was back in the cabin. He swallowed painfully—a reminder that the consciousness had been squeezed out of him. Thick smudges of dried dirt crusted the heels of his shoes.

"We know you're in there, boy!" Another pound on the door, and this time, Grey saw it wiggle inside the frame, bending to the frantic motivation of whoever was behind it.

"Sheriff's Department! Open up or we will breach!" That confirmed it. Sheriff Bobbit in the flesh.

But why was he trying to get in?

As Grey motioned to push himself up, something slick wiggled in his hand. He struggled through his warped vision to determine what it was.

And his brain caught up quickly enough to tell him that he was holding a bloody kitchen knife.

"Ew." Grey ripped his fingers away from the handle and rubbed them furiously on his pants. "Shit, shit, shit." That bad language resolution would need to be put on pause until he figured out whose blood he was smearing on his—

Oh no ...

Someone sat at the kitchen table, slumped over and completely still. Grey's eyes traced the body upward, from the muddy feet to the pajama pants to the wide-eyed and frozen face of Johnson.

"Johnson? You okay, buddy?" Grey asked.

But then a thin wake of blood flowed over the edge of the table closest to Grey, answering the question on Johnson's behalf.

Grey finally climbed to his feet. "Oh shit oh shit oh shit."

"Alright! We're comin' in!" Sheriff Bobbit yelled.

Grey was unconcerned with the Sheriff. Once he'd seen the gash on Johnson's throat, he couldn't pull his eyes away from the gradual outpouring of blood escaping from it.

"Johnson ..." Grey said under his breath, wishing he could simply sweep the blood back in and patch up the wound.

Sheriff Bobbit muttered behind the door, "Ya'll got your bodycams turned on, right?"

Bodycams, Grey thought. *The bodycams that were just dropped off at the station earlier today.*

In an instant, everything became clear to Grey. The bodycam footage would be edited into the film. *He* would appear on screen as the one who murdered Johnson and be gunned down by an overzealous yet heroic police force. *He* would be the new acolyte working behind the scenes with the Witch. It was almost too perfect. Made too much sense. The way he was found in the forest. The way he gained the crew's trust.

This was a trap.

The payoff to a setup Grey didn't realize he was a part of.

A twist.

Rodney, who had just revealed himself to be an absolute psychopath, never wanted Grey to get out. He wanted to make him a central part of the film.

"On three!" Bobbit commanded. "One! Two! Three!"

Smack! The front door shook again, this time with a little more give from the hinges.

Best case scenario: they'd make it in with two more hits.

Worst case: it would only take one.

Grey had to think fast before the hillbilly sheriff figured out how to count past one again. He had to stay out of view of the body cameras. Had to make it out of this house and get away from the body. But he knew he'd be chased by the Sheriff and his goons ...

So he'd have to lead him to a spot only *he* knew about.

"Please be there, please be there," Grey said as he ran toward the table adjacent to the front door, expecting another *thud* to project shards of wood and weakened hinges his way at any moment.

Yes! The keys to the van were still there where Larry left them.

"One!" Bobbit yelled.

Grey snatched them up.

"Two!"

Grey booked it toward the sliding back door and pulled it open.

"Three!"

He hopped out as the door exploded off the frame behind him. His feet mashed against the grass as he made his way around the corner, knowing good and well that there was no use in being quiet. The testosterone-soaked shouts from inside the home would silence his movement.

Grey made his way down the side of the house, then peered into the front yard. Three police cruisers in total. Two on the grass, one behind the van. It appeared as though he'd have enough space to swerve the van onto the grass and whip past the half-assed barricade.

Only one way to find out ...

With the keys gripped tightly in his hand, Grey sprinted for his life, blues and reds flashing across his face and carving his path. He didn't turn to check on the boys in blue—one small turn of his neck could slow him down. He needed to get to that van ...

He tried to plant his foot in the grass as he rounded the front bumper of the van, but his foot gave out and sent him into a full baseball slide. He tried to make it to his feet quicker than he should have, resulting in a Scooby-Doo-style wind-up with his legs. Frantic, Grey didn't *reach* for the driver's side handle so much as land on it. He pulled himself inside in a couple of quick moments.

His butt landed in the seat ...

The key hit the ignition ...

Grey looked up ...

Inside the house, uniformed officers growled and trotted through rooms, turning on lights and flipping over furniture.

None of them had any idea that he was there in the van, and with that realization came a long exhale.

But in order for his plan to work, they needed to follow him.

One small breath.

"Okay, boys ... Let's do a car chase."

Grey cranked the engine, and it sputtered to life. The headlights beamed into the house, blinding the officers inside. He put the van in reverse and mashed the accelerator. The van's tires dug into the grass as he zipped past the police cruiser behind him. The bottom of the van gave a metallic *screech* against the pavement as it skidded off the curb.

Before turning, Grey took a moment to take in the image of the frenzied police officers running excitedly toward their vehicles, waving their arms and shouting profanities, warning him to get out of the car NOW!

Adrenaline surged as if a match had lit within him. Because this was a mothereffing high-speed car chase.

Wait till Michael hears about this.

He put the van in drive, swerved around, and punched the gas pedal again.

No way could it outrun the police cruisers, but it didn't need to. He had a straight shot and a clear road leading to his destination.

Leading to the void.

THE CHASE

CRUNCH! THE BACK TAIL light smashed to bits against the hood of Sheriff Bobbit's cruiser.

The rear tires screeched as Grey struggled for control of the wheel. "Are you serious, man?!"

It should have been here by now ... Grey thought. *Just a little bit further ...*

The external speaker boomed from Bobbit's car. "We have high-powered rifles in our possession. If you do not pull over now, we will use them!"

The van only went to 110 mph, and Grey was giving it everything he had, revving down the empty road, all the while thinking it couldn't end like this.

This couldn't be the final chapter.

As if he willed it into existence, that dark, empty cloud appeared on the horizon like a hole dug straight through space and time.

"Come on, baby! Just a little bit more!" Grey yelled.

"You've left us no choice!" Bobbit said through the speaker.

All four vehicles approached the void rapidly, and Grey could only assume he hadn't heard a gunshot yet because Bobbit was too mesmerized by the floating scar of warped reality stretching like a black border around the town.

"That's right," Grey said. "Keep driving. Come get me, Sheriff."

Closer ...

Closer ...

Until the van was swallowed whole by the mouth of the void.

The town of Hope Hollow shrank in the rearview mirror as Grey, once again, found himself surrounded on three sides by an endless darkness. An infinite container with no floor and no ceiling. A space off the map where no one thought to travel. All the while, the police cruisers kept following, their sirens blaring and echoing across the dead space.

When Grey was satisfied with the distance between him and town, knowing it wasn't too far away to turn back, he slowed the van to a stop, and the engine sputtered like it needed a well-deserved rest. It wasn't long before Sheriff Bobbit swooped out of his cruiser, prompting his minions to do the same. The gang surrounded the van, six in total, guns at the ready, with one deputy making good on that promise of an assault rifle. They formed a horseshoe around the hood, and Grey wished he could take a snapshot of the looks on their faces captured in the headlights, their gazes floating back and forth from Grey to the nothing surrounding them, wide-eyed as if they'd all walked in on their parents having aggressive, passionate sex. It was especially satisfying to see the bewilderment slathered on Sheriff Bobbit's formerly smug face.

"What is this place?!" Bobbit yelled, the possibility sinking in that he hadn't chased Grey there, but rather that Grey had lured him there.

"You're in my jurisdiction now," Grey answered calmly, knowing Bobbit wouldn't hear it. It was gratifying all the same.

A groan sounded from behind the sheriff.

Bobbit spun, holding his revolver high. "Sheriff's Department!"

Another groan.

Slap ... Slap ...

The deputies turned as well, standing shoulder-to-shoulder with their leader and awaiting whatever came in the distance.

One groan became many, until the wet slaps of liquified feet became too loud to hear the groans.

"What the hell is that, boss?" the deputy with the assault rifle said.

"Fuck should I know?" Sheriff Bobbit answered.

With the combined glow of the van's headlights and the police lights still flashing, the outline of the approaching army materialized into view. First, it was the white, milky eyes.

Then, the browning teeth.

Then, the blackened, wet skin sagging from the skeletons of the poor souls trapped in the void.

A hundred bald, goopy figures marched toward them like a drunken, demonic army.

"Holy shit!" one of the deputies shouted, holding his sidearm more firmly as it shook in his hand.

Grey pressed his hand against the horn—*BEEEEEEEP!*

The horde rushed forward, appearing as one giant mass of decay as they willed their broken bodies toward the sound. Gunfire cracked through the void but did little to deter the onslaught.

Grey looked to his left and saw that the army would soon flank the officers. They were so focused on mag-dumping what was in front of them that they wouldn't know what was coming from the sides until it was too late.

Grey put the van in reverse, looked to his right, and paused.

A face he wouldn't have welcomed as friendly a day ago stared back at him through the passenger's side door. As the red and blue lights swiped across the vagabond's face, with his wiry beard and one eye having faded to near-total white, he gave Grey a smirk and a nod.

Grey nodded in return and pressed on the gas again, trading paint with one of the cruisers as he drove backward.

Away from the screams and muzzle flashes.

Back into Hope Hollow.

If the plan for the crew was to have them waste away in the woods, there might still be time for Grey to get to the Witch's house before they did.

There might still be time to roll into town and get reacquainted with the locals.

He took a look at the gas meter. The red hand was still at Full and didn't waver. He chuckled. "Figures."

Grey would need a full tank if he was going to orchestrate the best found footage movie ending ever.

His next stop was the only bar in town.

The Witch of Hope Hollow
Timecode: 01:02:13:58

Blaire sobs as she carries the camera. Exhausted, she's gone from a crazed run to a wobbling walk through the rainy forest.

She pants. Sobs. Pants. Sobs.

The camera light leads her way as raindrops worm down the lens, obscuring the passing trees.

"Johnson!" she yells. "Larry! … Caleb! … Are any of you out here?!" She whimpers. "Please …"

There's a *stomp* against the damp woodland floor behind her.

Gasping, she spins.

Nothing. Just branches and leaves wagging under the weight of rainwater. Then …

Shink … *Shink* …

"No," Blaire mutters.

She spins again. "Oh god no!"

The site of a butcher knife congealed to the stump of a man's hand causes her to leap backward. A large, stocky figure stands before her, wearing a cream-colored apron smeared with blood. He wears a black leather mask that covers his entire face, with only two openings for each wide and anticipatory eye.

She turns and sprints, screaming through hurried breaths.

The screen glitches in reds, purples, yellows, greens.

CUT TO

Blaire, sitting against the base of a tree, points the camera lens upward at her face. Raindrops bounce off of it, warping her matted hair and frightened, disheveled appearance.

"I don't know how long I've been out here. It feels like it's been days, but the sun hasn't come up. At first, I thought I was hearing my friend screaming, but … everywhere I go, he seems to get farther away. I think I might be going crazy. Is any of this even real?" She laughs crazily before melting into a crying state again. "His name is Johnson.

Theodore 'Teddy' Johnson. I think he might be dead. My friends and I went out looking for him, and we got separated … I hope they're not dead too …" She pauses for a few seconds. "If anyone finds this … do not come to Hope Hollow. This place is … evil."

A scream. Then, a voice in the distance yells, "Blaire!"

She looks up. "Oh my god, that's Johnson." She stands. "Johnson!"

She turns the camera forward. Runs.

More disorienting shakes and glitches cloud the screen as she yells, "Johnson! Where are you?!"

The camera continues shaking, capturing fragments of grass, trees, and darkness.

She stops with the camera pointed at the grass. "What the fuck …" She raises the camera to reveal a stone house in a clearing with moss worming up the sides; a house that appears to have been dormant here for ages, embedding itself in the earth, having become one with the forest. "Is that …" She lets out a heavy breath. "No, it can't—"

"Help!" Johnson screams from inside the structure.

"Oh my god." She sniffles, then lets out an agonizing shriek. "Johnson!"

"Blaire?! Blaire, I'm in here!"

She attempts to steady her breathing through sobs. "Fuck … Okay, I'm coming."

CUT TO

Larry bangs the iron rungs of a broken window. "Blaire! No! Johnson isn't in here! Don't come! Stay out there! We need to get out!"

Panting from behind the camera, Caleb says, "What's she doing?"

"She's coming in," Larry says. "Shit."

"It's good that we found her, right? Or that she found us?" Caleb asks. "We can all work on getting out of this house together."

Larry slaps his hand against the stone. "No, you don't understand. There *is* no getting out of here. We've been trying to get out for hours. It's a trap. We are *never* leaving this place." He grips the sides of his head, pulling at his hair.

"Don't say that, man. We're gonna get outta here and we're gonna show the world. For Isabelle."

"Izzy won't give a fuck about the movie! This was never about the movie! None of it was supposed to go this way!"

"What are you talkin' about? What's this all been about, then?"

A blue glow lights the stone hallway, reflecting off of Larry's glasses. "Oh no, no, no, no. Oh shit … It's time. We need to find Johnson. W-we need to find him now."

"What?" Caleb spins with the camera, refocusing on the end of the hallway where the blue light is creeping in, shining brighter. "It's time for what?"

"We can't go in there," Larry says from behind Caleb. "She needs three."

Caleb spins back around.

A figure stands hunched over behind Larry; hunched because the stone hallway can't contain the length of its bony arms and its backward legs.

A wide, yellow smile hovers above Larry's head and the epicenter of the crooked bones.

Caleb gasps as Larry stands frozen, feeling the presence of Willie Long Legs mere inches away from him.

Willie parts his teeth, and in a high-pitched voice says, "Time to play."

The screen glitches.

Caleb and Larry sprint away from Willie and into the bright blue light.

THE LURE

WITH THE ENTIRE POLICE force swallowed by the void, Grey trotted through the ransacked cabin, looking for any equipment the crew might've left behind. For what he was planning, they needed angles—lots of them.

Larry had told Caleb to bring everything he could carry.

He was happy to find that Caleb hadn't taken *everything*.

Grey knew he needed to get Elvis and the gang to the stone house. In a town as small as Hope Hollow, the truck wasn't difficult to find. It was parked outside the only bar in town.

Grey didn't know exactly how his plan would shape up as he mosied into the Thirsty Turtle; he just remembered the threat Elvis had left him with like a dark trinket for safekeeping.

If Elvis saw Grey again, things wouldn't go Grey's way.

And Grey was counting on him making good on that promise.

He noticed one of Elvis' goons sitting at the bar with a sweaty beer bottle, swiping through his phone. Bowl Cut. Either the dumbest of the group or the most confident, judging by the hairdo. Grey was willing to bet it was the former.

An idea formed. A stupid one, yes, but a stupid idea in lieu of a good one.

Grey nudged a bystander into the man, who dropped his phone and knocked over his own beer.

Then, Grey promptly swept up the phone in one swift movement.

He side-stepped the ensuing tussle and walked calmly toward the exit.

"Hey! That guy's got my phone!" Bowl Cut yelled, trying to untangle himself from the drunken mess of limbs and machismo inside.

"Come get it, pussy!" Grey shouted.

He spotted Elvis in the crowd just as a look of recognition crossed the unfortunately-named young man's face.

While Grey was being a little piece of shit, he might as well revel in Elvis' fury.

Grey ran outside, keychain in hand, and made a deep stroke of copper on paint across the side of Elvis' truck.

Elvis had sprinted out just in time to see the end of it. "What the hell are you doing? My–My truck!"

From there, it was another high-speed chase with a full tank of gas.

THE WITCH'S LAIR

As long as Grey stayed north, he'd find the house. He'd found it by accident once; surely, he could find it again. He hoped he could keep his legs under him with sheer grit and determination, but that was proving to be an incredibly dumb idea. The bag slung around his shoulder was slowing him down, and if the weight of the equipment wasn't bad enough, the rain didn't help at all. Hopefully the stuff inside wasn't too wet. He'd need everything to work out perfectly.

Also not helping: the small mob at his back getting increasingly closer. He'd put plenty of distance between himself and Elvis' squad when he stopped the van at the edge of the woods, but they were closing that distance fast.

With his lungs close to bursting, Grey willed himself forward, making sure the wand of Michael's compass stayed waving around the "N".

He caught a glimpse of glowing light beaming through the woods.

"Oh, that's gotta mean something," he muttered.

The stolen phone rang in his hand. Elvis' ugly mug appeared on the screen. Grey accepted the call and put the phone to his ear, panting into the speaker. "Kinda busy here. What's up?"

"Bro, where the fuck are you going?" Elvis asked on the other end. "Stop being a candyass, take your tampon out, and step up."

"What's wrong?" *Huff. Huff.* "You afraid of the Hope Hollow Witch or somethin'? You know that's just a myth. I'm just really scared that my face is gonna have to beat up your hand again. Honestly, me running away from you is, like, for *your* safety, not mine."

Up ahead, the source of the glow took shape. As Grey came closer, he knew he'd reached his destination.

The Witch's Lair.

He spoke into the phone. "Yeah, you know what, I'm done running. You're gonna see a house up ahead. I'm in there. Just follow the sound of my voice."

Grey ended the call and pulled a breath deep into his chest, shouting into the sky. "I'm heeeeeeeerrrrrrre!"

The Witch of Hope Hollow
Timecode: 01:05:24:37

Heavy breathing trickles in from behind a shaking camera.

Blaire scans the exterior of the stone building with her free hand as rain trickles down it. “Door … Door … Come on, come on …”

Finally, her hand touches wood. She steps back to reveal a thick brown door with a circular handle.

“Blaire!” Johnson yells from the other side of the door.

“Hang on! I’m coming!” Blaire yells back, throwing her fingers against the metal handle and pulling.

As the door parts from the stone wall, a pane of glowing blue light knifes through the opening.

“What?” Blaire whispers.

Johnson shouts again, this time, more drawn out and high-pitched: "Blllaaaaaai-iiirrrrre!"

She grunts as she pulls the door open, the blue glow expanding.

With the door fully open, she peers into the bright opening, filling the camera with a blinding blue sheen, and takes a few heavy steps inside.

All sound drowns out. No rain; just a *wom-wom-wom* like feedback on a speaker.

"Johnson!" she shouts.

The blinding light fades to a glowing arched door frame at the corner of a large room. Two figures stand on the stone floor between Blaire and the door.

Blaire's breathing intensifies. "What the fuck…"

She steps closer to the two figures. "Larry? … Caleb?"

She circles around them to the front, capturing their blank, frozen faces, eyes wide and cloudy, staring into the door.

"Guys?" she whimpers.

The door she left open slams shut beside her. She turns.

Having pulled it shut, a young woman in her twenties with matted brown hair and a pink shirt steps away from the door. She turns to Blaire with a menacing glare.

"Who are …" The question gets caught in Blaire's throat. "Holy shit. You're … You're Larry's sister."

Isabelle steps forward and opens her mouth. Her voice forms a deep, scratchy pitch. "Three souls for my three beautiful children."

Blaire's breathing quickens. "Nononono."

Isabelle speaks again. "Perhaps you should know why your companion Larry brought you here. The purpose you were meant to serve." Isabelle tilts her head up. Gasps.

Larry exhales, springing back to life and shouting, "W-what?! What?!"

Blaire turns the camera to Larry, who backpedals, knocking against Caleb. "Oh shit, oh shit, oh shit. I shouldn't be here." He sees Blaire, then spots Isabelle and leaps back. "Isabelle! Oh my god."

Just as he's about to step forward, arms raised, Isabelle grins. "You've been a very naughty boy, Larry. Haven't you?"

"Larry, what the hell is going on?" Blaire asks, whipping the camera from Isabelle to Larry.

Larry fixes his frightened eyes on Isabelle. "You said she'd come home with me. Let her go. Please."

"I said three souls for my three children," Isabelle says. "And you brought me three … including you."

"No, no, you already got Johnson! You have two others here!"

"What the fuck, Larry?!" Blaire backs away.

"Johnson isn't here," Isabelle said. "He's at your cabin resting in an eternal slumber." She giggles. "You were never leaving my woods."

The glow of the door intensifies.

The Witch laughs through Isabelle.

SMACK!

A thick branch hits the side of Isabelle's face.

Down goes Isabelle.

THE SISTER

GREY HAD SWUNG SO hard he'd figured the branch would break. But it was still intact, though he couldn't say the same for the cranium of the woman with a maniacal, otherworldly laugh now lying unconscious on the stone floor.

What in the fudge is going on here? Grey thought.

Caleb was frozen in place.

Blaire was aiming a camera at him and shaking.

Grey diverted his eyes away from the door sprouting light at the corner of the room. "Is that the glowing door?! You all know not to stare at that door, right? Have I been the only one paying attention? That old woman *literally* told us the glowing door puts you in a trance."

"What the hell did you just do?!" Larry shouted. "That's my sister!"

"Oh shoot, uh..." Grey dropped the bag, looked down at...

What was her name?...

"Oh, Isabelle," Grey said. "Good thing we found her, huh?"

Blaire's voice trembled. "Grey? Where have you been? Have you seen Johnson?"

"Oh my god, *who cares* about Johnson?!" Larry shouted.

Grey shook his head. "I'm sorry, Johnson, he's ... he's dead. The Witch's acolytes killed him and set me up for murder."

"Fucking *WHAT?!*" Larry exclaimed.

It was a side of the professor Grey hadn't seen before. Usually calm and collected, the man had lost all sense of cool, seeming less like a leader and more like someone who'd step on a few necks to get out of this house.

"We don't have a lot of time," Grey said. "We need to hurry."

Grey marched over to Caleb, wincing at the surrealness of his glowing eyes. "Yo! Caleb!" He snapped his fingers. Clapped his hands in front of Caleb's face. "You don't ..." *Snap.* "... stare ..." *Snap.* "... into the door." *Clap.*

Caleb remained unmoved.

Grey sighed. "Sorry about this, dude." He cranked his arm back and swiped an open palm against Caleb's cheek.

Caleb recoiled, stumbled, then fell to a knee, holding his cheek. "Ow! What was that?"

"Grey hit you," Blaire answered. She looked over at Larry, who was cupping Isabelle's head and patting her cheek. "Right after he knocked out Larry's sister, who I'm pretty sure is the Witch, and oh my god, what the hell are we still doing here?!"

"Larry's sister is here?" Caleb said.

Grey bent down to Caleb. "Buddy, we gotta make some moves, okay? I brought your security camera equipment over there in that bag." He pointed. "It was under your bed, just like you said it was. The hotspot, all of it. It's all there. We need to get this set up now. Is it really as simple as turning on the cameras and the hotspot?"

Caleb shook his head. "Uh, yeah. It'll automatically connect and upload to cloud storage."

Grey stood, directing them with his hands like an orchestrator. "Everyone grab a camera. Place one in each corner and make sure you're getting the center of the room."

"Can't we just leave?" Blaire asked.

"The Witch wants three souls, right? I got three on the way."

A growl echoed through the house, causing the foundation to rumble under Grey's feet.

Grey hopped over to the bag and unzipped it. "That must be the Witch. She must be getting antsy. She wants her souls *now.*"

The Witch of Hope Hollow
Timecode: 01:06:18:15

Cut between three angles of the stone room—corner view, corner view, corner view.

A glowing door, upright and secured to nothing, stands at one the corner of the room.

"Where you at, little bitch?" Elvis walks into the room.

Freckles follows closely behind. "Yo, what is this place? I feel like we shouldn't be here, man."

"Don't be a pussy!" Elvis shouts. "Dude's tryin' to … spook … us …" He trails off as his eyes become transfixed on the glowing door. His pupils fade until his eyes display the same color as the glowing door.

"Elvis, you good?" Freckles asks.

Elvis's voice deepens with a long, demonic drawl. "Looooook."

"Look at … wha …" Freckle's eyes lock onto the door. His body tenses. His eyes cloud.

Bowl Cut stomps inside, knocking into Elvis. "Where's my goddamn phone?!" His eyes land on the glowing door. "Whoa, what the shit is that?"

His trance broken, Elvis shakes his head and stands, shouting, "Where are you?!"

Bowl Cut gasps. "We shouldn't be here."

"We'll leave as soon as we find that car-keying asshole," Elvis says.

"Do you seriously not know what this is?" Bowl Cut pleads.

"Yeah, that little prick set up a glowing door to mess with us," Elvis replies. "Hey!" He trots over to Freckles and punches him in the chest. "Quit playin' around!"

"How in the hell would he have done this, Elvis?!" Bowl Cut shouts as Elvis shakes himself out of the spell.

"It's obviously fake." Elvis speedwalks over to the door. Grips the handle. "I'll show you."

Bowl Cut yells, "No! Don't!"

Elvis opens the door.

An explosion of blue light plasters the room as Elvis's body bends backwards, head folding onto heels, a force sucking him inside by his midsection so quickly it cuts off his scream like an axe chopping wood.

Elvis was there a second ago. Now he's not.

Bowl Cut shields his eyes from the light.

Freckles freezes in place, once again succumbing to the power of the light.

"Fuck this. I'm out." Bowl Cut turns to leave through the door he came in from.

Shink … Shink …

"Oh god…" He backs away.

Entering the room and matching his footsteps is the Butcher, dragging his machete hand against the stone frame as he appears.

From an opening in the corner of the room, slender fingers wrap along the wall. The smiling face of Willie Long Legs squeezes through—first his long arms, then his crooked legs.

Bowl Cut grabs Freckles by the shoulders. "Wake up! Wake up!"

Freckles steps forward, walking slowly to the door.

"Stop!" Bowl Cut yells as he attempts to pull his friend back.

But Freckles keeps walking, undeterred.

"Shit!" Bowl Cut removes a pocket knife from the back of his pants as the Witch's children converge on him with slow, menacing movements.

THE WAY BACK

"WE NEED TO FIND a way out," Grey said, leading them through the stone hallways of the building.

Blaire and Caleb followed behind, holding their cameras, as Larry grunted with Isabelle cradled in his arms.

"The house is a maze," Caleb said. "It seems like we've been here for days. We have no idea how to get out."

"The Witch was just buttering you up. Warping your perception to try to break your minds," Grey replied. "She's got Elvis and his construction crew to nibble on now. We should be able to get out."

"What? How'd you get them here?" Blaire asked.

"By being an annoying little prick," Grey answered.

Larry panted. Wheezed. "Hey, none of that shit was true. I just ... had to play along to get us out of there. You believe me, don't you?"

"How is your sister here, Larry?!" Blaire shouted. "Pretty hard to believe anything right now."

"What are you guys talking about?" Caleb asked.

"I'm pretty lost too, my guy," Grey answered as he skimmed the stone wall with his hand, watching as a shattered window frame appeared with a view of the woods on the other side. *If we just stick to this side, we'll make it,* he thought.

Come on, come on ...

The corridor opened up into a large room with unlit candle fixtures placed around a staircase. Finally, there was a door to the outside.

"Here!" Grey yelled, motioning for them to move faster and reaching for the door.

"Is this the goddamn door we came through?" Caleb asked.

Grey ripped the door open and held it. "Yeah, it's magic. Whatever. Let's go."

But when he looked through the open door, a man with a ripped black shirt and matted black hair stood on the other side, soaked in rain and haloed in moonlight ten feet away in the mossy front yard of the Witch's mansion.

"You can't leave," Rodney said.

THE VILLAIN

"GET OUT OF OUR way, *Rodney*," Grey responded, stepping into the rain.

Blaire came through behind him, shining the camera light on Rodney. "Who the hell are you?"

"What are you gonna do?" Rodney asked, stepping forward. "This is my world. I will not let you ruin—"

Blaire took hard steps toward Rodney.

The disheveled man stuttered. "W–what are you—"

He was silenced by a shattering of glass and metal as the front of Blaire's camera collided with his nose. He grabbed his face, wailing in pain.

Blaire raised the camera like a club. "I am so sick of being in these ..." She swung downward. "... WOODS!"

The second blow did it. The third was for good measure. Rodney was down for the count. The hits couldn't have been enough to kill him. But Grey was willing to bet they were hard enough to keep him down—to keep him from getting his perfect ending. Grey didn't give a rip what that meant for him. Not anymore.

"Do you know who that was?" Blaire asked.

"Remember I told you about that local guide that was showing me around the woods?" Grey replied. "That was him."

"Really?!"

"I guess these woods just have a way of making people go nuts."

Larry and Caleb dragged Isabelle's body out and laid her on the wet moss. Larry fell to the ground and cradled her head.

"Izzy," Larry said, stroking her thick clumps of hair. "Izzy, it's me. It's Larry. I got you."

Caleb stepped toward Rodney, the fallen stranger. "Who's this?"

"Just some psycho," Grey said. "Blaire clocked him with the camera."

"Damn, Blaire. Is the footage still salvageable?"

Blaire held up the camera and inspected it. "Body's still intact."

Caleb let out a sigh of disbelief. "This is gonna be one hell of a documentary."

"Don't celebrate until we're out of this fucking town," Blaire said.

Grey studied Rodney's bludgeoned face, thinking it was the best he'd ever looked. He wondered if he'd see him again on the other side, though Grey knew that getting back to the real world was still up in the air even for him.

If we do meet again, Grey thought, *I'll shatter every bone in my puny little fist against your face.*

"Is it true what you said about Johnson?" Larry asked Grey. "That he's ..."

Grey took a moment to respond as the image returned to him—Johnson leaned over the dinner table, eyes wide, blood dripping down from the corner like spilled paint. Real or not, Grey had seen it, and it wasn't something he could ever unsee.

"Yeah," Grey said. "He's dead. I'm sorry."

Larry sniffled as he rocked his unconscious sister on the ground. "Blaire, Caleb, I ... I'm sorry. I'm so sorry I brought you out here."

"I'm sure you didn't mean for this to happen," Grey said. "We need to move."

"No." Blaire put a hand on Grey's chest, halting him. "You don't understand. Me, Caleb, Johnson, we were never supposed to leave here." She gave Larry a stern look. "We were pawns. You knew exactly what we were walking into. You were just playing dumb this whole time. Every time you told us we should go out into the woods, you were just hoping we'd get lured into this trap. Three souls for the Witch and you get your sister back. The math checks out."

"Wait, what?!" Grey exclaimed.

"What?" Caleb followed.

Blaire hovered over Larry and Isabelle. "Tell me I'm wrong. By God, I *really* wanna hear that I'm wrong about you right now."

"I can explain." Larry took a deep breath—another second that Grey felt ticking off the clock.

Grey interjected. "Let's explain later, yeah?"

"He was going to sacrifice us, Grey."

"So you never cared about the movie?" Caleb asked. "Damn, man."

Grey put a hand on Caleb's shoulder. "You wanna spite this guy? Make it to the end and finish the movie. Drive far, far away from this town right now."

THE DEPARTURE

Michael's compass pointed south. Grey's sneakers were fully soaked after thousands of steps through the soggy mix of leaves and dirt. He thought very intentionally about removing his shoes and socks, as his feet were getting heavy, as when he'd almost gotten to the tipping point, ready to plop down and say to hell with it, the van and Elvis' truck appeared side-by-side.

"Yes!" Grey shouted. He turned back to Blaire and Caleb. "You get in the van and you drive. Your clothes and equipment are already loaded up. *Do not* go back to the cabin."

"Aren't you coming with us?" Blaire asked.

"No, I have to tie up some loose ends. Is Larry still behind us?"

Blaire looked back. "He should be."

Grey slid open the door to the van. "The keys are already in there. Go."

Blaire wrapped her arms around him. "Thank you. For everything. It seems unfair that Larry got his sister back and you didn't."

Grey wanted to stay with his cheek to hers for a moment longer. He longed for the warmth of her embrace, but in a way he hadn't felt before. A platonic friendship. He wished they could stay in touch.

He wished he could keep tabs on Caleb's career as a documentarian.

In the aftermath of such horrors and absurdity, Grey began to realize that he would actually miss the film crew.

Grey parted from Blaire, looked her in the eyes, and said, "Blaire ... thank you. Really."

She smiled, then climbed into the driver's seat.

Caleb, staring down at his smartphone, put a hand on Grey's shoulder. "Dude ... it worked." He looked up at Grey. "All the security footage uploaded. This is going to be groundbreaking. This isn't even about an MFA program anymore. I'm going straight to the front of the line. This footage ..." With no more words left to convey his gratitude, Caleb gave Grey a hug. "This is incredible. Did you just save this entire project?"

"Go make movie magic," Grey said. "For Johnson."

The small glimmer of excitement faded from Caleb's expression. He nodded. "For Johnson." Caleb slid open the van's side door and stepped inside.

Larry emerged from the woods, panting, knees wobbling as he did a fireman's carry with his sister.

"Come on." Grey waved him over. "You don't deserve a ride out of here. I wouldn't be surprised if they changed their minds."

Larry hobbled toward him. "Could you help me, please?"

Larry bent and tilted, and Grey let Isabelle fall into his arms. She was tiny—couldn't have weighed more than a hundred twenty pounds, but when she sank into him, Grey realized how tired his own body was.

"My bad. You know ... for knocking her out," Grey said. "You know she was possessed, right? At least, that's what it sounded like."

Larry flashed a sad gaze at Grey. "If anyone can understand why I did what I did, it's you. You're looking for your sister, too. What would you do to bring her back?"

He'd phrased it the wrong way, but Grey rearranged the words himself. It was a reminder that everything he was doing was to get back to Cassandra. To get back to Michael. Grey was the one who was lost and had to fight his way back.

"Try to take care of yourself," Grey said.

Larry climbed into the van, then, with Grey's help, began pulling Isabelle inside. Neither Blaire nor Caleb seemed too keen on helping with the exchange.

From the driver's side window, Blaire said, "Come with us. Like it or not, you're a part of this crew now. We can get you back home."

Grey's cheek arched into a grin. He really did feel like a part of the crew, but he knew this was the end of the line. All he could do now was wait, and the pit in his stomach yearned for a visit to Martha Mae's diner.

"I still have business here," Grey said. "Just make sure people know what happened in Hope Hollow. All of it."

"Come on, man," Caleb pleaded.

Blaire sighed. "How do we find you when we get back? You don't even have a phone."

"Don't worry," Grey said. "I'll see you on the other side."

Grey slid the van door closed and patted it twice, then marched off toward the truck, hoping the keys were still inside.

The van's engine cranked behind him. The wheels sputtered in the mud before they gained traction.

The van backed up, turned, and drove out of the clearing and off into the night.

It wasn't until Grey climbed into the driver's seat of the truck and let his body sink into the cushion that he realized just how exhausted he was.

The crew was gone.

The movie was finished.

Grey's hope that it would all be over soon tapped in his heart while the yearning for his new friends—ones he wouldn't see ever again—squirmed in his stomach.

This was a fitting ending.

Wasn't it?

The Witch of Hope Hollow
Timecode: 01:09:32:11

The crew bounces with the motion of the van as it rolls over grass and dirt, then makes its way to the main road. They all sit quietly as Blaire presses down on the accelerator.

Caleb aims the camera at Blaire and says, “Watch your speed, yeah?”

“I *am* watching my speed,” Blaire snaps back.

“Sorry … Just don’t want to give Sheriff Honky-Tonk any reason to stop us while we’re within the town limits, you know? At the same time, though …” He pans the camera to the side window, where a blur of never-ending trees zips past the vehicle. “... I can’t wait to get away from these damn woods.”

"I'm sorry too," Blaire says. "I feel like I'll be myself again once this town's behind us."

"Yeah, you kinda bludgeoned a guy with a camera lens back there."

"Uh-huh."

Caleb points the camera at Larry in the backseat, which is still folded out like a bed. Larry cradles Isabelle in his arms.

"You got anything to say, Larry?" Caleb asks.

"Get that camera off me," Larry says without looking away from his sister.

"How 'bout that," Caleb responds. "This entire weekend, you've been barkin' at me to film everything. Now you're getting camera shy?"

"You don't know what it's like." Larry looks up. "To have that Witch in your head. To never have a moment's rest knowing she might appear in the corner of your room. To hear the screams of your lost sister every second of every night. This was the only way I could get her back. The only way I could make it stop. If you could just try to understand … maybe in time you could forgive me."

"Forgiveness is gonna be hard to come by," Blaire calls out from the front of the van. "The only reason we're alive to forgive you is because your plan didn't work."

"Yeah, dead folks can't forgive," Caleb says. "You would've had your sister back, and we would've been stuck here, right?" He grunts. "Well, congratulations, Professor … You wanted to be the star of this movie; you definitely earned that."

"We need to talk about this footage," Larry says. "No one's going to believe the shit that's happened here—"

A soft voice quiets him. "Larry?"

Larry looks down at Isabelle, now fully conscious. His breath catches in his throat. "Izzy?"

"You … you found me," Isabelle says.

Larry sniffles. Whimpers. Nods.

"How long?" Isabelle asks.

Larry strokes her cheek. "God, Izzy … Too long … But it's okay now. I got you. We're gonna be okay—"

A groan erupts from deep within the woods like a giant horn embedded in the foundation of the earth. The ground shakes beneath them.

"What …" Caleb gasps as he whips the camera back to the side window. Light pierces through the trees in bright, endless streaks.

"Shit!" Blaire screams. "What now?!"

Twenty feet ahead, a figure emerges from the woods, sprinting frantically.

"Blaire, are you seeing this?" Caleb asks. "Is that ..."

As the figure comes closer, his appearance is made clear. It's one of Elvis's goons, waving his arms in an attempt to flag down the vehicle, bowl cut bobbing toward them.

"The Witch needs three," Caleb says.

THE SLICE

Grey was happy to see that the diner was open. When he'd pulled up, the interior lights glowed as if to display this metallic monument of nostalgia.

Armed with the eleven dollars and change he'd taken from Elvis's glove compartment, he pushed open the steel door. The diner was empty, save for Martha Mae, who gave him a warm smile from behind the counter.

"Good to see you survived, what with that Witch out there and whatnot," she said sarcastically, raising her eyebrows.

She had no idea how honest that sentiment was.

Grey chuckled. "I didn't get to try that cranberry pie last time I was here."

"I knew you'd be back for it. Why don't you take a seat? I'll heat a slice up for you."

Gladly, Grey obliged and lowered himself onto a swivel chair at the bar area. The drive from the woods to the diner had allowed the lactic acid to seize around his legs. Everything below the belt was tight.

"Where are the rest of your friends?" Martha Mae asked.

"Left town early." Grey hoped they were long gone by now.

"So I'm guessin' this is your last night here?"

I hope so, Grey thought before replying, "Like I said, just had to try the pie. I'm really hoping to get back soon."

"I'll get you filled up and on your way. I don't mean to pry, but ... looks like you got a lot on your mind. Just you and me here. Anything you care to talk about?"

So much, Grey wanted to say as his thumb skimmed the compass in his pocket. Instead, he told Martha Mae, "There are two people I really miss, and ... this is gonna sound weird, but I have this feeling I might not ever be able to tell them *how much* I miss them, you know? Like I had all of these opportunities to tell them how much I loved them, and I just ... didn't. I think it might be too late now."

"Oh, honey," Martha Mae says. "It's never too late to tell someone you love them."

Grey took the compass out of his pocket and inspected the new battle scars on the brass casing.

"I feel like I've been on this treadmill, and they've been begging me to get off. Maybe this place I'm finding myself in now ... maybe it's like a—What do you call it? Purgatory? I'm finally starting to feel like maybe I deserve it."

Grey looked up at Martha Mae, then quickly looked away. The sadness on her face shot a punch of guilt in his gut. Whether she was real or not, the empathy seemed genuine, and Grey was *really* bringing her down.

"I'm sorry," he said. "Just feeling a little introspective, I guess."

Martha Mae flashed that warm smile of hers. "This is the place to do it. I'll be right back with that pie. Don't look now, but it seems like someone's about to crash our party."

As Martha Mae walked to the back of the diner and out of view, Grey swiveled in his seat tepidly.

The door swung open ...

And the unwelcome, bruised and gashed face of Rodney appeared. Clumping, greasy hair clung to his shoulders. Water from the soaked fabric of his shirt dripped down to the floor.

"You," Rodney said.

"Rodney?" Grey set the compass down on the counter. "How did you even get here?"

"That—" Rodney stepped forward. "—is not—" Another step. "—my name!" He raised his hands like they were heat-seeking missiles having just acquired a target: Grey's neck.

Grey swatted his hands away, but Rodney's pursuit was too strong—too crazed. And before Grey had a moment to react, his back was flat against the countertop, feet dangling, and Rodney was above him, bearing his teeth and spewing foam from his lips like a rabid animal.

The ground vibrated beneath them. A strange, deep groan emitted through the town as if Hope Hollow had awakened from hibernation and was now angry and famished. Light flooded through the windows of the diner.

And yet Grey didn't have much of a chance to pontificate on why exactly that was happening. The pressure on Grey's windpipe? Yeah, that was Rodney's thumbs digging into his neck. For such a scrawny little man, Rodney had a grip that could turn a screw on a rusted junkyard vehicle.

"The movie's ... over," Grey said, choking on his own words.

"Three souls!" Rodney screamed. "She needs one more! I'm giving her *you*!

The Witch of Hope Hollow
Timecode: 01:11:06:43

Caleb swivels the camera toward the source of light.

Larry presses himself against the back doors as glowing yellow spears sprout from Isabelle's eyes like high beams on a highway.

"That's not Izzy!" Caleb yells. "Definitely not Izzy!"

Isabelle rises from the makeshift bed, hovering in place. Her neck tilts too quickly, prompting an awful *CLICK* of bone as the beams in her eyes flare into Caleb's camera lens. Her cheeks rise into a crazed smile. A booming laugh echoes from deep within her.

Beneath the suspended body of Isabelle, the makeshift bed melts down into the metal, down into nothing, slowly being replaced by glowing strips of wood.

Forming a glowing door.

Isabelle says into the camera, “Three … souls.”

The side door slides open behind Caleb.

“Get out of the van!” Blaire shouts.

Caleb spins and leaps out, then sprints down the open road.

His camera catches a glimpse of Bowl Cut just before he stumbles in place in a clumsy attempt to reverse course.

“Where are we going?!” Caleb screams.

But Blaire doesn’t answer.

Larry gives a pitiful wail, begging them to, “Wait!”

Caleb spins the camera just as Blaire closes the van door, closing in the light.

Closing in Larry.

“What are you …” Caleb trails off, knowing the answer before finishing the question.

Blaire books it away from the van.

Larry screams.

And screams.

And screams.

The light inside the van grows like a solid mass.

Blaire shields her eyes.

Everything goes white.

Until the light disappears. There one second; gone the next.

With the light gone, so too are the screams.

The only thing audible is a chorus of panting as Caleb and Blaire catch their breath.

"Holy shit," Blaire says. "Is he …"

"Yeah," Caleb says. "I think the Witch just got her third."

They stand for a few seconds, taking in the sudden calm that's spread through Hope Hollow.

Blaire says, "You know I had to … right?"

"Uh …" Caleb responds. "I think I can edit that part out."

THE COMPLETION

Darkness closed in on Grey's vision, tunneling around that wet, ugly mug of Rodney. His hands slapped at Rodney's slimy, scrawny arms that were locked at the elbows, trying to pry them off but unable to catch a grip.

CHKK-CHKK.

Music to Grey's ears. Martha Mae coming to his rescue again.

He rolled his eyes back and was delighted at the upside-down view of Martha's Mae's hand on the pump of her shotgun.

"You get outta my diner *now*, boy."

But Rodney didn't flinch. He kept his eyes on Grey and grinned. A drop of foam fell from the edge of his lip and onto Grey's cheek. "You wanna know how I got here so fast? Huh?"

A cinematic *SMASH* of glass stung Grey's eardrums. Splinters of broken window slapped against his dangling legs.

A flash of hardened skin, white fabric, and feathers ziplined overhead. Even in a glimpse so brief, Grey knew it was that thing that had first greeted him. That hellspawn with the sewn mouth and bulging eyes—the one he'd impaled and left for dead.

Lady Hyne, Larry had called it.

But *Lady* implied royalty. And there was nothing majestic about the talons aimed at Martha Mae's screaming face.

POW! Martha Mae got off one shotgun blast before bird-woman's claws found her skin, and the two of them screamed together painfully, tumbling far into the back of the diner.

Rodney was looking away from Grey now, gleefully admiring the carnage. Either Rodney had lost it in this place or he was always this far gone.

Maybe he really *was* meant for Hope Hollow.

Grey's hand searched the counter for anything he could use to pry Rodney off of him. A fork? A knife? Heck, even a spoon?

But then, that smooth, round surface graced the pads of his fingers.

Brass.

Glass.

Michael ... I'm comin', buddy, Grey thought as he gripped the compass; a compass thin enough to fit through the small opening in Rodney's smile, right between his teeth, though Grey wasn't delicate with his insertion. The object packed enough force to chip Rodney's two top teeth on the way in.

Rodney eased up, gagging on the circular item obstructing his airflow.

Grey bucked, slamming his heels into Rodney and forcing him to the other side of the diner.

Rodney's backside landed on glass, and he squealed.

CHKK-CHKK-POW!

Grey sat upright and flipped his head back to Martha Mae, who wore a fresh coat of blood across her face, neck, and chest. A floating array of feathers slowly descended around her like fog. The dead demon bird at her feet told Grey the blood wasn't Martha Mae's.

So much for the cavalry.

The light that plastered the windows dissipated like a million bulbs dying at once.

Martha Mae and Grey stared at each other for a long couple of seconds, gathering their wits, while Rodney reached into his mouth, digging for the compass.

Martha Mae took a breath and wiped blood off her chin. "You good with that one over there?"

Panting, Grey shrugged. "Yeah, I think I'm good."

"I'll be right back with that pie." Martha Mae cocked the shotgun again and turned as an empty shell landed next to Lady Hyne.

A perplexed chuckle escaped Grey's lips as he watched the woman disappear to the back once again.

The saliva-covered compass landed with a *CLANK* at Grey's feet. Rodney grunted, struggling to pick himself up off the glass-covered floor and baring his two chipped teeth.

"Why do you hate me so much?" Grey asked. "What, because I got your name wrong once back in high school?"

"Because they listened to you!" The words came out slurred. "Because every time we got around to brainstorming a new idea they went straight to you. I never got a chance to speak."

"That's got nothing to do with me." Grey crouched down Rodney's level. "I spent a long time blaming other people for my circumstances. Now, before today I would have looked you in the eye and said, you? ... You were a shy kid. You can't blame other people for talking over you when you couldn't talk for yourself. I'd encourage you to find the courage to face your shortcomings that I didn't have before all of this. But now?" Grey pursed his lips. "Now I see you're just a crazy piece of garbage."

The red and white paint behind Rodney began to shift, almost like the wall was glitching. The first time he'd seen his surroundings glitch in that uncanny manner, Grey's mind couldn't make heads or tails of it. Now, the abnormality was completely rational—Welcome, even.

A swell of hope grew inside of him, for this abnormality meant that he could be going home.

"And now it looks like you're gonna have to answer for what you've done in the real world."

The booth seats flickered around Grey, sliding into digitized ribbons.

Taking in the psychedelic shift as well, Rodney muttered, "No no no no no ..."

Grey scooped up the compass, then placed it in his pocket.

"She needed three!" Rodney screamed. "It can't be over!"

"What can I say?" Grey responded. "You went up against a heck of a crew and lost."

"What? What crew? What are you talking about?"

"*My* crew."

The smell of cranberry pie preceded Martha Mae's footsteps. Grey turned to her as a vortex of pixelated light swallowed the diner, placing the entirety of Hope Hollow in a blender and swirling it around.

Somehow, before all the colors of the unreality had congealed into a white mass, Grey's ear caught one last kindness from Martha Mae:

"You take care now, honey."

THE REALITY

ALL OF THE MATTER in Grey's body had been scrambled and pieced back together.

At least, that's what it felt like when every atom in his body vibrated back into place like a demolition in reverse.

Faint and gloomy orchestral music greeted him in his new environment. His eyes adjusted to a slow cascade of white letters sliding down a black screen.

Credits.

He'd forgotten how dingy the theater had smelled—the popcorn butter, the dusty seat fabric, the spilled soda gone sour—and yet he welcomed it, even as the aroma of the theater competed with something equal parts savory and sweet.

Sitting pleasantly upon a small saucer held up by Grey's thumb and index finger was a slice of cranberry pie, practically glowing in the dimly lit room.

"No!"

Grey knew that voice.

"Nooooo!"

A hand struck the top of a seat three rows down from Grey.

Rodney, still wet, still petulantly angry, pulled himself upright. "I wasn't supposed to come back! I'm not supposed to be here!"

Rodney raced toward Grey with his jagged teeth, but it was a different approach; one that didn't read as aggression. Rodney carried that wide-eyed bewilderment of a man stranded on an island, spotting a boat in the distance, and begging for rescue.

"How did you do it?" Rodney pleaded. "How do we go back?"

Speechless, Grey scanned the sticky floor for the camcorder ...

And there it was: Sitting on the aisle carpet, lens aimed at the screen.

Rodney followed his stare and said, "That's it, isn't it? The camera—that's how we got there." He rushed over to the camera fiendishly and hovered over the object with reverence, his hand gliding over it as if to not desecrate its immense power.

Grey knew he should've taken the opportunity to smash his wimpy little fist into Rodney's quivering jaw. The man had put him through hell after all. But he decided instead to leave Rodney in the theater. To leave him in this strange, primitive state. An angry, lost soul pining for a way back to his life of artifice.

Rodney could have that life if he wanted it, Grey reckoned. He could finagle and twist his way back into that place he preferred.

Grey, however, was happy to be back in reality. Weird, confusing, harsh reality.

"How do I start it? It–it won't turn on!" Rodney muttered as Grey continued walking away, stepping into the aisle and heading for the double doors.

He pushed the doors open, welcoming light into the theater, and was greeted by a young kid—sixteen if he had to guess—in a glittery silver vest holding a broom and dustpan.

"How was the film, sir?" the boy asked.

"Uh ..." Grey giggled and kept giggling, knowing that he looked like he was high and wondering if he actually was. His knees were about ready to buckle, his throat was still sore, and a piece of still-uneaten pie that was birthed from another world was calling to him. "It was a wild ride."

Getting a closer look at Grey, the kid lowered his voice. "Why are you wet?"

The doors burst open behind Grey. Rodney bumped into his hip, nearly causing Grey to drop the plate.

"Ryan?" the boy said.

Rodney clutched the video camera to his chest. With his tattered, soaked shirt, matted locks of hair, and impossibly wide eyes, he looked truly, utterly possessed. "Projector booth," he said. "W–we need to restart the movie."

Rodney sprinted away toward a corner of the building, his sneakers making sloshing noises as he went.

The theater worker looked from Rodney and back to Grey. His jaw hung open, searching in vain for words.

"You know ..." Grey took in a mouthful of pie and kept talking. "... I was warned before I watched this movie that it made viewers go crazy. Like it's cursed or something." He shrugged. "You guys should use that for marketing." He swallowed. "Oh, also, that guy admitted to poisoning his father and trying to kill him. Multiple times, actually. I lost my phone. Could you call the police? I mean, you saw the guy—Ryan, is it? He's clearly not right in the head."

The kid's eyes widened in horror.

And that was the final thing Grey said as he left. Martha Mae's pie was as good as advertised. Too good to waste on words.

THE AMENDS

GREY STOOD IN FRONT of Cassandra's door for the second time that evening.

There shouldn't have been a second time. He never should've left.

It's why he didn't bother to run home and change. Didn't so much as find a paper towel to mop up his hair. Grey wasn't *Grey* anymore. He was a new Grey who had battled demons and outsmarted a witch and an overzealous lawman, all so he could be standing in front of this door again. He didn't want to waste another second—that's what *old* Grey would do.

But in his mad dash to get back to the apartment, he realized he hadn't had a chance to collect his thoughts. Never mind that it was nearly ten o'clock and past Michael's bedtime.

He was starting to think he'd need to save his guts for spilling tomorrow morning when Cassandra's voice traveled from the other side of the door. "Why are you just standing there like a weirdo?"

Grey's cheeks flushed. "You can see me?"

"Yeah, I heard you walk up. What do you want?"

"Uh ..." There it was: That brain scramble he wished he'd taken the time to smooth over. There was a lot he wanted to say. Too much to say all at once. So he started with, "I've been a really bad brother."

Cassandra grunted. "Grey, not tonight—"

"No, no, really. This isn't a pity party. This isn't me feeling sorry for myself. This is me telling you I want to do better. I *will* do better. For you. For Michael. I promise. You might just get sick of me helping so much."

"Who's that?" Michael said from behind the door.

Though Michael's voice was muffled, it put a smile on Grey's face all the same.

The door opened, and on the other side of the threshold was a very annoyed Cassandra next to Michael, bouncing giddily in his superhero pajamas.

"Buddy," Grey said, "you're up late."

"I just saw the trailer," Michael said. "That's so cool!"

Grey laughed. "What trailer, buddy? What are you talking about?"

"He got a ping on his iPad before you got here," Cassandra said. She turned to Michael. "Which *should not* have been in your room." She rolled her eyes and turned back to Grey. "Some movie trailer account he follows posted a new video. He came out of his room and showed me. It definitely looks like you in the trailer, but I had to break it to him that you're not an actor."

"Wait, what?" Grey cocked his head. "What movie?"

Michael darted off to his room, and for a few awkward seconds, it was only him and that stern stare of Cassandra, to whom he mouthed *sorry*.

Now equipped with an iPad, Michael came running back to the open door and yelled, "Look!" As his mom shushed him, Michael handed the device to Grey.

On the screen, below the rectangular display with a large play button at the center, the text read: The Witch of Hope Hollow - Trailer.

"No way ..." Grey whispered.

He tapped the play button.

Ominous text faded in and out on screen, detailing when and where the events he was about to see took place. And then, familiar faces came to life on screen.

Blaire.

Caleb.

Johnson.

And, of course, Larry, looking much more confident—pompous even—than when he'd last seen him.

An abrupt cut in the video displayed the rough terrain of the woods, lit only by the circular glow of the camera.

"Hello? Sir, are you okay?" It was Blaire's voice.

Ten yards ahead, a haggard man held up a hand and mustered a hoarse response. "Wha ... What?"

And Grey realized he was staring at himself.

"It's you, right?" Michael said. "Mom didn't believe me."

Grey paused the video, inspecting the still frame before him—that days-ago version of himself shielding his eyes, with a fresh cut on his midsection.

He couldn't hold back his smile. His cheeks raised in a way he hadn't remembered them doing so before—at least, not in a long while. The muscles around his lips, jaw, and cheeks relaxed as if awakened from a long-dormant state.

Grey's eyes shifted to Michael.

"Boy, oh boy, do I have a story for you, buddy."

Acknowledgements

I was nine years old at the time *The Blair Witch Project* was released. Thanks to a brilliant marketing campaign, it was the first time I can remember being scared at the *concept* of a film.

Because it felt real.

It wasn't until many years later that I actually saw the film. I will never forget the feeling of watching Mike facing the corner of that dark basement in the final shot of the film.

As a 90s kid who grew up shooting silly movies with a DV camcorder, I love that there's an entire subgenre of horror that can play to that nostalgia while also giving us a good scare. I've watched and loved so many found footage horror movies, and to see the format continue to launch promising careers for many filmmakers warms my heart. And speaking of ...

How freaking cool is it that Anthony Cousins blurbed this book? I consider *Frogman to be* a found footage horror masterpiece, and I'm incredibly grateful to Anthony. I can't wait to see where his career in horror goes moving forward.

Of course, I have to give thanks to Josh Powell, with whom I originally conceived of this idea. One day, we were going back and forth talking about how funny it would be to make a found footage movie that pokes fun at the tropes of found footage horror. I went off and wrote a book with those ideas in mind, and I hope some day filmmaker extraordinaire Josh gets to make the movie version.

As usual, Josh is always my alpha reader and the one who encouraged me to move forward with publishing this book. Thanks, dude. I'll see you in like, five minutes, probably.

Big thanks goes to Rebecca White for a much needed developmental edit. Rebecca greatly improved this book. I can honestly say it's much better because of her input.

Thank you to Nico Bell, who is the best editer I know. I am a much better, more confident writer than I was before I met her.

Big thanks also to these folks for reading early versions and providing extremely helpful feedback as well: Bryan Farrell, Alex Esarey, Leanne (@fetidpages).

Thank you to A.D. Aro, Marissa Yarrow, T.T. Madden, Jesse from Jesse's House of Pulp, and Abby Wolf for the amazing advance blurbs! It's great to have talented friends, isn't it?

I want to thank Amanda Powell, of course, for putting up with my interest in horror and tolerating the films that inspired this book.

And thanks to YOU for reading this far. I hope you enjoyed the ride!

–Joey Powell

About the Author

Joey Powell, "renaissance man of horror" (Horror, Humor, Hunger Podcast), is a publisher, editor, writer, and artist based in North Carolina. He is also an actor and frequently collaborates on film projects with his writer/director twin Josh Powell.

He can be found on social media as @wowcooljoeywrites.

His long-form works include:

Night Games (co-authored by Josh Powell)
Nightmares From the Gray
Squirming All the Way Up

www.ingramcontent.com/pod-product-compliance
Lightning Source LLC
Chambersburg PA
CBHW020021180826
50006CB00033B/590
* 9 7 8 1 9 6 6 4 9 7 2 8 8 *